FLEMISH FOLKTALES RETOLD

BY SIGNE MAENE
WITH A FOREWORD BY
KERRIA SEABROOKE

ILLUSTRATED BY CATE ZEEDERBERG

Gatto Books
First Edition
2024

Dedicated to all the beautiful souls
who supported our project

CONTENTS

FOREWORD

My first encounter with the fantastical world of Flemish folklore was two years ago when I ran across a series of intriguing social media posts by the Belgian author Signe Maene. Her lore-filled capsules gave me a glimpse into the magical folklore of Flanders in the northern part of Belgium, where Dutch is the first language.

Though I had never met these characters, they seemed somehow familiar. Throughout my childhood, I spent many hours poring over stories in the antique book *Richard's Topical Encyclopedia, Volume 14*, and a vintage copy of *The Original Folk and Fairy Tales of the Brothers Grimm*, absorbing the greater truths about the world that emerged like jagged rocks from the harsh tales. Signe's folkloric stories are inhabited by similar grim and grisly kindred spirits that creep from her interpretations, such as Kludde, a sinister shapeshifter, the deadly vengeful witch, De Roesschaert, and the pernicious gnome-like Alvermannekes. Even the more zany characters such as the baleful ghost, Flabbaert, the mad giant, Lange Wapper, and Lodder, a terrifying trickster, are not the sugarcoated folklore characters we often encounter today but are angst-ridden creatures that will stop at nothing to achieve their desires.

Ensconced in my own world of cross-platform story-telling, what first struck me about Signe's posts was the timeless quality they had, and, like most of her readers, I found myself wanting to know more about her world of Flemish Folktales. I appreciate her singular passion for the dark characters that she deftly plucks from the distant past, polishing them until they once again sparkle, enchant, and often threaten to kill you. As Signe and I became friends, I was charmed to learn about Signe's rare collection of folklore books and her endless search for new, old, forgotten Flemish tales. When she approached me with the idea of *Flemish Folktales Retold*, I immediately agreed—this was a book that must be written.

With great delight, I accepted the invitation to edit her collection of folklore stories. Over the past few months, as we've worked together on her book, I've had the hair-raising pleasure of romping through haunted Flemish forests, enchanted meadows, and treacherous bodies of water. These dark and twisted tales are populated by an outrageous cast of outcast witches, shapeshifting toads, werewolves, evil ghosts, phantom dogs, cats, men of the cloth, and delightfully murderous hares. These folklore figures lurk in the old-world Flemish land filled with creeping cynicism and deadly superstitions, where revenge is whispered around every corner, and betrayal seeps down to the very roots of the ancient cursed forests. Signe's landscapes are painted with a fine brush that depicts an eternal sense of farms, villages, and forests yet leaves much room for her twisted embellishment of the subtle layers of emotion and the startling voices given to the often silenced outcasts and demons.

These stories have been retold lovingly, with all sympathy falling decidedly on the dark side. There is little grappling with redemption as these characters grab you with their clawed hands and drag you into a world howling with relentless injustices. In the Lord of Misrule tradition, these dark beings feel the world is brutally unfair and wield every scrap of power they can scrounge to right the wrongs they feel they have been dealt in this topsy-turvy dimension.

Gone are the safe worlds of The Smurfs—instead, we travel back in time to a nightmarish realm where superstition and fear ruled the starkly elegant forests and villages. No place is safe from the relentless undercurrent of terror and dread. There are no saccharine, sycophantic princesses flouncing across these unsanitized pages. Signe's fiends are often outcasts out for blood—and succeeding more often than not. *Flemish Folktales Retold* serves us a buffet of cautionary tales: Beware if you dare mess with the powers of evil. Yet, this cast of creatures retains a level of humanity that echos our shadow selves. Their outrage at the unjust world tugs at our heartstrings, and we inwardly breathe a sigh of relief that we might never have the terror of meeting one of them while strolling through our own world.

It has been a thrilling experience working on this disparate collection of supernatural tales that date back to a time when storytelling was a verbal art, and audiences believed in the power of superstition. I endeavored to be as invisible as a ghost as I traveled respectfully through these thirty-six folktales while appreciating their ancient origins and Signe's loving crafting of each tale. While her characters may be heartless, Signe Maene has put her heart and soul into this darkly dazzling collection of stories, illustrated with the gorgeous and haunting art of Cate Zeederberg.

I invite you to read *Flemish Folktales Retold*, filled with a macabre cast of Flemish characters just dying to meet you!

WITCHES

WITCH IN THE DUNES

"Why would I eat your fingers? I have no argument with you, and even if I did, there are tastier things in the world than fingers," said the witch.

"But you do have an argument with my father. Would you eat his fingers?" the girl asked.

The witch sighed as she continued to bandage the young girl's fractured wrist.

The girl had been in this world for thirteen years, and the very first thing she ever remembered being told was to avoid the dunes. Yet, here she was. In the dunes. And even with the fierce wind twisting knots into her thin hair and the sound of the waves singing a calm but wildly menacing melody, she could hear her father's stern voice: *Don't go near the hag's cottage.* Yes, she could hear his voice even here, but there was something quite mesmerizing in the way the sand swirled around the witch's long black dress, which made her think that her father must be wrong.

"Your wrist will heal. Leave me alone now." the witch said. She had used a strip of tree bark as a splint and wrapped her wrist in the torn fabric of what had once been a pillowcase.

Only twenty minutes before, the girl had been hiding from the wailing witch. The sorceress had a wicked and sinful soul, at least that's what they said in the village, and that's why she decided to run when the witch walked in her direction. She was convinced that the witch would cut off her fingers and eat them. Then, the girl had gone and tripped. She thought that was the end of her. But the witch didn't cut her up or boil her in a cauldron along with snake tongues and owl wings, and that's what the girl didn't understand. Why would such a malevolent soul take care of her? Why did she still have all of her fingers?

"The storm destroyed our cottage, too," the girl said in an attempt to console the witch. Not a single house in the village still had a roof. Timber, broken cabinets, and glass lay scattered over the streets, and the storm had claimed the life of more than one sheep.

"I would grieve for your father's loss as well as my own if I didn't have to watch him throw what remains of my wicker chair on a bonfire."

The girl turned around and looked at the familiar town that had now become unrecognizable. When the news reached the villagers that the witch's cottage had been destroyed, they all rushed to the dunes and grabbed what they could find. The girl had been with them. Not because she wanted to steal the witch's belongings but because she had never been allowed to go to the dunes before.

"That's what you need to do if you want to be accepted?" the witch spat on the ground. She watched as the villagers tossed the mangled shutters she never opened on the fire while they shouted: *Burn the witch.* The shouting intensified as her books were thrown into the flames. *Burn the witch. Burn the witch. Burn her.*

"My father's going to build us a new home," said the girl, watching tears roll down the witch's shriveled cheeks. After a long pause, the girl noticed a strange glow in the woman's eyes. For a moment, she thought that the moon dwelt in her pupils along with a storm, a storm much more terrible than the one that had just destroyed their village.

"Did your home have irreplaceable books that were centuries old?" the witch asked, "Or clay dolls crafted by your great-grandmother? Crystal stones in which a power resides that is stronger than you and I?"

"No," the girl said while the villagers continued to scream,

Burn the witch!

"Your father will rebuild his home," the witch said, "and once his warm and cozy house is finished, I will raise a storm. The wind will be vengeful and destructive. Rain will flood every cellar and every street and turn your beloved market square into a lake. The lake will have beautiful waves, waves that will be wild, hostile, and deadly."

"Spare my father, please," the girl said, "I know you don't hate me, or you would have eaten my fingers. Please, don't do it."

"Enough with the fingers, you silly girl," the witch said, "I am De Roesschaert. I have never bothered anyone. I never left my beautiful home, but now all that is dear to me is gone. I will capsize the boats of those who are toasting my loss. I will cause suffering in the guise of a ferocious cat to feast upon those who are now feasting. I lost the most precious possession of them all: my home. I will terrorize this town and become its worst nightmare, ha!" the witch's cackle froze the blood of all that heard it as she walked toward the sea. She waded into the salty water without looking behind her and slowly walked further and further out until, at last, she disappeared.

***

The girl ran to what was left of her village. She understood the witch, but she didn't want her father to build a new home only to see it destroyed. She wanted to tell him everything that had happened, but he had already fallen into a deep sleep next to the scorched pyre as he murmured *burn the witch*. The whole village slept beneath the stars that night, but the girl was wide awake.

The next morning, she told her father everything that had happened. He scolded her for talking to the witch and then scolded her again for being so gullible. It was obvious that the witch had drowned herself. Soon, a spontaneous feast broke out. The villagers danced in the rubble as they sang, "*The witch has drowned*," while two small boys handed the revelers a cup of ale. The girl noticed the boys were just as confused as she was. How could a storm that had destroyed so much and left them with empty stomachs cause so much happiness?

Then, with no warning, terror arrived. In the shape of a cat, De Roesschaert appeared and attacked those who had thought her dead. The villagers were covered in scratches and bruises, bite wounds and lacerations. The witch tore holes into boats and sank every ship. She raised storms the likes of which even the most hardened sailor had never encountered on the high seas.

Years later, after they had rebuilt their village for the fifth time, a man at last arrived who knew what should be done to rid the village of De Roesschaert. He proclaimed that all the fishers should be baptized for a second time with seawater, and each one should receive a new name. Once this had been done, the witch finally ended her reign of terror. The young girl, who was now a grown woman, was grateful that there were at least some sunny years ahead.

THE LAST LETTER OF SEFA BUBBELS

Tell me, is someone knocking on all the doors in the village to let the people know that there will be dancing and rejoicing around a bonfire tonight? Has someone told the innkeeper that he will sell more beer today than on any of the feast days? Are you smiling as you stare at my gray and bloated corpse? Tell me, are you covering your nose because my body is releasing a putrid stench into the air, or can you still detect that woody fragrance I was known for? You might as well tell me. I know that you, who are reading my last letter, did not mind talking about me while I was still walking on this earth. Whoever told you that the dead can't hear was lying.

I had a family once. Years ago. Did you see me after my husband and five children succumbed to the plague? I remember I was shaking when I chopped a snake into pieces and rubbed the parts on their fevered bodies so that the evil disease would crawl back into the serpent. When that did not work, I looked for leeches underneath stones near the creek, but my family died before the slimy worms could fill themselves with bad blood. Did you see me then? When I was alone? Did you see me when I was sleeping on the streets with my feet wrapped in bandages because they were covered with chilblains and blisters? Did you see how dry and chapped my hands were, turned blue by the cold? All you offered me were meaningless words, but did you give me a blanket? No. A cup of ale? No. Bread? No.

Only after I moved into the hovel at the edge of the town did you begin to see me. But did you really? See me? No, you feared me. I had vowed to avoid everyone who lives in this cursed town, but I soon found that I was no longer alone. I was surrounded by friends. Thirteen of them. Owls. They wear a cloak of soft feathers, nothing like the mud-spattered, itchy cloaks you all walk around in while wagging your venomous tongues.

But even though I shunned you, I have always seen you. I see you just as clearly as an owl sees a mouse digging in a field while night reigns over this town and snatches that little pest up before it has the chance to flee. There may be many things you think you can escape from, but there's no escaping the talons of an owl.

But why am I telling you things you already know? I taught you that lesson! That night, when my owls summoned all the sister witches in the area, none of you closed an eye. One of my sisters suggested gauging them out. I told her to bring me a pair of scissors, but when I held the pointy steel in my hand, I changed my mind. How would you have seen ghosts riding through the black evening sky, leaving blood-red trails of mist behind them without eyes? Or the swarms of rats gnawing at your wooden houses until they wobbled? Or the uprooted trees dragging you from one side of the village to the other? You needed your eyes to witness that night of dreadful bliss, and I hope that a feeling of horror engulfs you each time you open them.

I withdrew again after that night of vengeful merrymaking. I read books, the titles of which would make you tremble, and poured liquids into bottles, the labels of which would ensure you never left your houses again. And the incantations! Ow, the incantations! The spells I tested on ants and flies would have stopped your heart from pumping blood.

Life is slipping away from me, and the devil will be here soon, but like my owls, the rest of my witches are here to stay. All of you have faith. Faith that you will be welcomed in heaven, but

even if that is true, my witches will ensure that you will rot here on earth. In this hell.

You think I'm exaggerating? Oh, poor you! See what happens when my coffin is loaded onto the carriage and transported to the graveyard. Women wearing hoods that cover their faces will appear. They will screech. They will wail. They will sing laments. Count them as they mourn me, for that's how many witches live here, and then think, think of all the havoc they will wreak upon your wretched souls!

DIE GNYDIGE

"Surely, you don't expect me to take you with me?" Goedele folded a dress and stuffed it into her suitcase.

"Why not?" Her husband asked, "You're not the only one who wants to leave this cursed town for a couple of days."

"Of course, darling, but not when it's Friday the 13th. The men stay in the village, and the women visit their families," she said as she opened the dresser drawer and grabbed her comb.

"Why? Where's the bloody sense in that?"

"You know very well why. Men have the courageous hearts of lions and are therefore strong enough to stay here, while we women are weak and faint at the first sight of blood. We wouldn't survive if we stayed. You don't want me to die, do you?"

"Doesn't mean that I can't go away too if I wish."

"It's tradition, darling," Goedele snapped her suitcase shut and stood by the door, "remember, there's broccoli soup in the pantry. All you need to do is heat it up."

Goedele silently hummed a song as she stepped onto the street. Tonight, this street and the whole village belonged to Die Gnydige. Oh, what a terror she was! The men called her 'old hag' in cowardly whispers as they didn't dare to confront her. She was a witch who often appeared in the shape of a cat. When Die Gnydige begged, the men always emptied their wallets for her, afraid that she would send an army of lice to march through their hair if they didn't.

As she left the village behind her, Goedele thought of what had happened yesterday morning. Her husband's screams had woken her up. There had been a cat sleeping at the foot of their bed. A beautiful black cat with bright blue eyes. It was Die Gnydige. Goedele had covered her mouth with her hand because she feared her husband might see her grinning as he chased the cat out of their house with a broom. He didn't stop shaking for the entire morning, not even after she dropped some laudanum into his tea. The poor thing!

Of course, she wasn't going to visit her family. Why would she? To play cards with her father and waste her time gossiping with her mother? No, Goedele was heading into the woods.

A number of women had already gathered around the Great Oak. They passed around a pipe filled with chestnut leaves, which they smoked as they chatted enthusiastically about what would happen when the moon appeared in the sky. After a while, Goedele leaned against one of the trees and drifted off to sleep.

When she awoke it was finally time. In place of hands and feet, she had grown paws and a tail, and sprouted whiskers on her cheeks. Goedele was now a black cat and she crept to the hole underneath the derelict house where Die Gnydige lived together with the hundreds of other women who had shapeshifted into cats.

The night was stormy with wind that blew in all directions and made the house gate creak. The inside of the hole was crowded with many jars that contained the bones of toads and squirrels. The ceiling emitted a phosphorescent blue light as glowworms crawled across the ornate plafond. In each corner stood a skeleton-like tree in which bats dangled upside down. The skin of a werewolf Die Gnydige had once stolen served as a carpet, but the most special object stood in the middle of the room. A huge cauldron surrounded by a cloud of dark blue smoke. Within the smoke, Goedele could see the screaming faces of all the charlatan witchfinders Die Gnydige had sent to hell, where they were forever trapped.

This Friday the 13th was an important day, for it was Die

Gnydige's 113th birthday. The witch of all witches had been teaching her sorceresses the dark arts for over a century now, and Goedele hoped there would be many blissful years to come. Die Gnydige herself floated through the room on a chair made from living, hissing snakes. Many of the cats scoured the age-old books while others purred, kneading pillows as they memorized the ancient spells.

"Ooh-ooh…" one of the cats cried, "There's something approaching."

"Impossible," Die Gnydige said, "All of my cats are already here, and the ghosts will join us at midnight."

"No, I tell you that I can see our husbands, brothers, and sons. They're heading towards the hole, carrying straw and torches. They mean to suffocate us with smoke!"

The cats gasped as Die Gnydige leaped out of her chair, sending the snakes tumbling to the ground and slithering in all directions.

"It seems they've had enough of burning consecrated candles to keep the so-called 'evil' that comes out of this hole at bay, eh?" Die Gnydige stood before her cauldron and gazed into the smoke, "Well…they may try, but they are never going to win. The witches are here to stay, and they'll have to learn how to live with magic. Otherwise…"

"But they'll kill us!" three of the cats shouted simultaneously.

Goedele felt like scratching the mewling cat's eyes out. How dare they interrupt Die Gnydige?

As the men outside lit the straw with their torches, A fearful hush fell over. Many of the cats flattened their ears and twitched their tails.

"Believe in your power as a witch and walk through the flames," Die Gnydige said as smoke started to fill the hole, "Believe in the magic that has gathered you here, for you are all strong witches, strong women, and strong cats."

The cats walked through the fire. The flames felt cold and seemed to strengthen the magic that lived in their bodies. They arrived unharmed on the other side of the ring of fire and chased their husbands, brothers, and sons deep into the woods. The cowards were terrified and didn't dare to return to the village.

The victory was supposed to be a huge celebration, but it had turned into a night of mourning. The cats were unharmed, but Die Gnyidge wasn't. She had given the felines the last of her magic so that they might live and become the next generation of formidable witches. Goedele and the rest meowed nonstop in sorrow, and when the ghosts arrived, they wailed with them. Even the devils who dwelled in the marshes and rivers and the specters who lived in the wind didn't laugh or sing that night, for Flanders had lost their dear, wicked witch.

The next day, the men returned to the village.

"What's that on your arm?" Goedele's husband grabbed her wrist, "Why are you burned?"

"Can't you tell?" Goedele laughed, "Oh, surely you must know now?"

"You're a…you're a witch."

"And you're a murderer."

After Goedele separated from her husband, she lived a witchy happily ever after while he continued to tremble until death finally allowed him to be still.

THE TOAD

I was an ugly child. I was an ugly woman. My green eyes were unsightly, my long cadaverous fingers were revolting, and my dry hair looked so horrible that even birds would not nest in it. How relieved they must feel! Those who called me hideous and unloveable. I won't be offending their eyes for much longer, for soon I will be dead.

It wasn't just the gamblers and drunkards who wasted their precious time in my alehouse by calling me ugly. My father called me ugly, my brothers called me ugly, and my mother... well...my mother said I was pretty while she pursed her lips together and stared at the ground. She was lying.

I was ten when I sat on a chair in our small courtyard garden and wondered what I had done to be cursed with such an unsightly and disgusting visage. Then, I noticed a toad crawling in the grass. I stroked its dry, bumpy skin and counted the reddish and black spots on its muddy, dark green back. The toad's eyes were a bright gold. They were powerful. Peculiar. Pretty. A veil of mysteriousness surrounded this toad, along with something wayward and cunning, something wicked and magical. It was in that moment it dawned on me that I would never be like the other girls. I was a toad, but I saw what others couldn't see. Beauty.

After that, I no longer cared if they called me ugly or fed me their lies born out of pity. I told myself that I possessed the rare kind of beauty only toads have, and I wanted to become one of them. I wanted my skin to be poisonous. I wanted to feast on slugs and ants with my sticky tongue, and above all, I wanted to be left alone. When I was sixteen, I snuck out of my home in the dead of night and walked many miles to a rock. I put my hand on the mossy stone and walked three times around it, singing a song worshiping the devil and his many names while I did so.

That night, I became a witch. I now had the power to shapeshift into an animal of my choice. While most witches were fond of cats, hares, and magpies, I chose the prettiest creature to walk this earth: a toad.

It was in this form that I crawled through forest leaves and walked on cobblestone roads to Bruges. There, I lived as a woman and worked as a seamstress while the sun shone. I slept in the woods as a toad when night fell. I didn't need my family, and I most certainly didn't need a husband. I did everything myself, and it was a blissful day when I stopped sewing and opened an alehouse. The place was always packed, and I loved how the silly guards of the city squandered all their money on playing cards and getting drunk.

Then, one day, something terrible happened. I was serving ale from behind the counter when a wealthy merchant strolled in. It was early in the morning, but apparently, the man didn't mind that my workers were still pouring buckets of water on the vomit last night's regulars had left behind or the sticky rings on the tables from where their pints had been. The merchant started with one drink, but by the time noon arrived, I wondered if he planned to empty a whole barrel.

Once darkness fell, the merchant had an attack of hiccups and could no longer stand on his feet. I was about to leave the alehouse in the hands of my capable workers and return to the woods for the evening when I heard him say he didn't have enough money to pay the bill. I couldn't believe my ears. He wore a waistcoat made out of the finest linen and had a golden pocket watch but didn't have enough to pay the bill? The man said his brother-in-law would drop by and settle the bill later, but I read dishonesty in his eyes. In fact, he didn't just stink of ale and sweat; he also reeked of lies and deceit. A knave in fancy clothes. I called him a scoundrel, looked him in the eyes, and told him that he wouldn't reach home tonight.

I shapeshifted into a toad and followed him through the streets of Bruges. Because the ale had turned him into a blabbermouth who thought everyone wanted to hear his life's story, I soon learned he had a boat in the canals that was his, and it would bring him home. I crawled into the boat. Oh! What fun that was!

He tried hard to unanchor his boat, but the boat would not budge. He asked some of the guards to help him. Big, strong men would surely be able to move this boat, non? Non! Ah, I was looking forward to watching him curl up on some street corner. He was about to have the worst night of his life. He would soon feel as if he was being strangled and suffocated, and even if he managed to fall asleep, he would be plagued by gruesome nightmares.

Unfortunately, that didn't come to pass. When the guards emptied the boat of the ropes, barrels, and oars, they found me. One of them stabbed me and flung me into the gray canal water. My golden eyes glowed like fire. I wanted to curse them, but I didn't have enough time to speak the words. The boat was free now, and they all climbed aboard that blasted crate of wood and continued to stab me in my stomach as I floated alongside the boat.

I didn't die right away. I still had some strength left and returned to the alehouse. I thought that shapeshifting back into my repulsive human form might save me, but alas! They pushed the tables of the alehouse together and laid me on the sticky wooden surface. One of the guards with whom I was on good terms heard that I was dying, and he ran to the alehouse. He turned white when he saw my wounds, for he now knew what I knew. I am a toad, and he was one of my murderers. The guard fainted. His heart was so horrified by his evil deed that it stopped beating. Now, the time has come for me to die as well, but I will not leave this world in my ugly human form. I will die as a pretty toad.

THE WITCH MUST DIE

"We need to talk about your mother," the priest said, sitting in one of the wicker chairs in front of the fireplace. He hoped he didn't have to stay any longer in this house than was strictly necessary. It wasn't the only drafty old home in the parish where unwelcome guests such as cockroaches and rats ruled the roost, but it was the only house where no crucifix hung over the door, and no Bible could be found.

"When will my sister be here?" Nelleke asked, "I cannot abide mother's moans, sobs, and wails for one minute longer."

"Your sister will not be coming," said the priest, "she would rather die herself than have anything to do with her mother."

"She's always been selfish," Nelleke leaned on the mantelpiece and buried her face in her hands, "what am I to do now?"

"Don't blame your sister. She's a god-fearing soul who has suffered much because of the evil acts your mother has committed."

"And I haven't?"

"Do you remember my last sermon?" The priest stood up. He didn't like that Nelleke's tear-streaked face loomed over him. The offspring of a witch, regardless of how innocent the child was, should never be above a man of the cloth.

"About how God wants us to be compassionate?" he continued when Nelleke didn't respond, "We have to forgive those who aren't strong enough, like your sister, and we have to forgive those who are evil, like your mother. That's what you must do now. Forgive."

"Forgive the witch?" Nelleke asked, "Have you forgiven my

mother for sending the mysterious wind that blew the roof of the church away? Or for the mist that turned all of the apples and pears in your orchard into a mushy mess? What about the time she…”

“She gave birth to you. Now you can give her something that’s much more precious: death.”

“I will not become a witch. You have known me my whole life, and I am offended that you think I would risk such a cruel fate and wind up in hell. I’m just as devout as my sister is.”

“Look at me, Nelleke,” the priest laid a hand on her shoulder, “look into my eyes. You will only be a witch for one day. Consent to inheriting the powers of your mother, and the devil will let her go. The agonizing pain she is in now will stop. She will die. And tomorrow, I will return and release you from those foul and unnatural powers.”

“Do you promise? Do you promise on all that’s holy?”

“I’m a man of God. Do you really believe I would suffer another witch to walk these streets?” he said, his hand already turning the doorknob.

“Very well then,” Nelleke said as she collapsed into a chair.

The priest closed the door behind him. He was relieved to breathe pure air again. Air that wasn’t poisoned by the stench of a witch. He was even more pleased when he realized that the sky, which God had created on the second day by separating the waters, would tomorrow be as God intended - without witches.

The next day, the priest rose earlier than usual. He said his prayers and relished every bite of the fried eggs the maid had prepared for him. He left the house when the birds were not yet done singing their early morning songs. The golden sunrise promised that it would be a beautiful day. It was a sign. *Thy will be done on earth as it is in heaven.* And his will, the only will that mattered, would be done, and it would be done today. He walked through the narrow street in which Nelleke lived and smiled when he realized that soon, every single house would have a crucifix hanging above the door.

"Ah, *mijnheer pastoor*, I wouldn't go in there if I were you," said a man with a wrinkled face and gray hair.

The man often sat on a chair in his small front garden, watching the happenings of the shoemaker across the street. The priest had seen this man many times before and had intended to visit him and ask him why he never attended Mass. But the priest hadn't gotten around to it yet.

"You need not fear the witch any longer. She is dead," the priest said.

"The old one is dead, aye, and she didn't die quietly either. Not even one of my eyes would close with all of that racket going on.'"

"You'll sleep well this evening." The priest assured him.

"If you do go in there, tell her to ask the devil to teach her those dark arts silently. I don't care a fig about the evil they brew or the ointments they make that allow them to fly through the sky. Who am I to tell someone what they can and cannot enjoy? All I'm saying is that they must do so quietly."

"Nelleke will be declining her inheritance. There will be no more witches."

"Ha! Tell yourself that as often as you like, *mijnheer pastoor*. I've been alive longer than you, and it's said that the witches' inheritance is worth more than the relic of the Holy Blood Thierry of Alsace brought to Flanders. It is knowledge beyond anything you can imagine. It's a gift given to those who are shunned by society and once they know how to perform incantations and curses they are no longer alone."

The priest folded his arms and tilted his head, "why do I never see you at church?"

"I'm an old sinner with only a bottle of brandy for a friend, *mijnheer pastoor*. Why would you want me at your church?"

The priest committed himself to paying the man a proper visit tomorrow. He would read The Bible to him. Reading the holy text to those who had lost their faith always reawakened the old love they had once felt towards God and sent them back on the path of righteousness.

A wry smile appeared on the man's face as he watched the priest knock on Nelleke's door. Nelleke answered. Her eyes were bloodshot, and her hair was disheveled. She wore a black mourning dress with lace ruffles at the sleeves and one of her mother's cabochon pendants with a dark purple stone. The priest had seen it before and had thought then that the pendant gave the devil eyes where he shouldn't have eyes.

"As promised," said the priest, "I'm here to set you free. God will be in your heart again. He will be closer to you than he has ever been before, for he loves those who make sacrifices to help rid this world of witchery."

"Go away," Nelleke said. If her eyes had been able to kill, he would have been dead.

"What?" he stumbled backward, "Nelleke, you are not the witch your mother was. The evil that calls your body its home can be vanquished. You can win this battle!"

"Go away," she slammed the door in his face.

The man on the porch laughed, "I told you so, didn't I?"

"Living next to a witch doesn't bother you at all?"

"Like I said, She may do whatever she likes as long as she does it silently."

The priest shook his head as he walked down the street. The sun had already risen, but it no longer looked like a beautiful day. Foreboding clouds hung in the air, predicting the disorder and turmoil to come.

HEDGES AND BUSHES

Annelies thought she was dreaming, but even her dreams could not have conjured such a frightful yet enchanting scene. Witches danced around an oddly shaped oak tree, cats meowed high in the branches, and ghosts flew into the air. Annelies gasped in amazement. Without warning, the ghosts descended and offered their arms to the witch who was standing nearest to them. The witches and ghosts proceeded to dance a dance she had never seen before. The ghosts lifted their partners up in their misty arms and tossed them high into the air before catching them and setting the cackling witches on the ground.

Annelies crept closer to watch as the revelers nibbled on plum cakes served by bats on plates made from the backbones of skeletons. They washed it all down with wine served in the hollowed legs of horses. She noticed that one of the tabby cats high up in the tree carried a wriggling rat imprisoned between its feline teeth. Another tiger cat frenetically clawed the tree bark in a way that made Annelies think it was completely mad. Then there was Midnight, with a red ribbon tied around his neck. He was swinging back and forth from one of the branches, his tail twitching to the sound of the hellish music played by some cats on out-of-tune saxophones, harps, and bongos.

Midnight? What? What was Midnight doing here amongst these witches? He was a tuxedo cat, with one of his paws a sock and the other paw almost entirely white. His muzzle was divided into uneven black and white colors. Annelies thought she was imagining things. She closed her eyes, but no! When she opened them again, Midnight was still there. He was her cat, and she had named him Midnight because of his habit of sleeping all day and only leaving his precious chair when night fell.

"Midnight…" Annelies whispered, "come here, Midnight." Annelies had forgotten that he never looked up when she called his name at home. Now, he reacted to her voice, but he stared at her with eyes so vicious that they could only have been born in hell. Unexpectedly, the music stopped, and Midnight wasn't the only one who now stared at her.

"What do we have here?" one of the cat witches asked.

Annelies turned and ran. She ran through the woods as quickly as she could, but icy, cold hands reached for her and grabbed her shoulders. The hands belonged to the ghosts who lifted her high into the air. Though she was impressed by how far she could see over the trees, she frantically demanded to be put on the ground.

The ghosts obliged, and Annelies plummeted earthward near the Great Oak tree. Once she tumbled to the ground, she was instantly surrounded by the cat witches she found appalling yet oddly fascinating at the same time.

"What's the meaning of this? Why are you spying on us?" asked the creatures.

"You have my cat," Annelies said, though Midnight acted as if he had never seen her before in his life.

"Your cat?" one of the witches scoffed, "your cat? What do you think, girl? That cats are your property? That they are here to obey your every whim and keep your feet warm at night? Cats only have one master, and that is themselves."

"He lives in my house. I feed him. I care for him," Annelies saw that they didn't believe her, "look," she said, "his fur is still on my dress."

"Be that as it may, cats own you, girl. Not the other way around."

"What are we to do with her?" one of the other witches asked.

"You tell us, Midnight," another said, "will she go over hedges and bushes or through hedges and bushes?"

Midnight climbed on the shoulder of the witch who had just spoken and whispered something in her ear.

"Through, he says."

All the unhallowed creatures narrowed their gazes at Annelies as they formed a circle around her. A chant escaped their lips.

Through hedges and bushes, door heggen en hagen, through hedges and bushes.

The murmurs grew louder and faster with each passing second

until a violent windstorm appeared.

Through hedges and bushes, door heggen en hagen, through hedges and bushes.

The witches clapped their paws wildly and cackled as the windstorm carried Annelies into the air.

Through hedges and bushes, door heggen en hagen, through hedges and bushes.

The chant no longer only seemed to come from witches and cats, but the trees, the hares, and the foxes seemed to sing along with them, making the windstorm grow stronger and stronger. As the wind carried Annelies away, she soared through hedges and bushes, their thorns scratching her skin so violently that Annelies felt as if the plants were not just living things but living things with a thirst for blood. She cried out for mercy, but they ignored her pleas. Eventually, she passed out.

The next day, Annelies awoke bloodied and lying in the grass at the edge of the forest. She thought of breaking a branch off a tree and using it as a walking stick to stagger back to her cottage, but she changed her mind when she recalled the stories she had heard of people doing exactly that. It was said that trees let out horrifying cries because of the ghosts that lived inside them.

After many hours, she reached her front door, and there Midnight was sitting innocently on the windowsill, waiting to be let inside. She petted him on the head and vowed to herself to never speak a word of Midnight's double life to anyone. She secretly wished that she, too, could dance with the ghosts of the forest and was pleased that at least Midnight went to magical assemblies, though she was resolved never to enter the woods again.

ENDNOTES

Alfons de Cock, one of Flanders's most important folklorists, notes in *Vlaamsche Sagen uit den Volksmond* (1921) that almost half of the tales he has collected are about witches. He writes, "Doesn't this tell us a lot about the people?" Other folklorists from the same era also note that the belief in witches and witchcraft is still very much ingrained in the Flemish culture. If you were to step into a version of Flanders that teems with the beings that haunt it, there would live a witch in every street, curses and spells would be spoken every five seconds, and there's a good chance that the cats, hares, rabbits, magpies and other animals you meet while walking the folklore paths are shapeshifting witches. Because of the large number of witch tales, it wasn't an easy task to select just six stories for this chapter. Ultimately, decisions had to be made, and the retellings aim to immerse the reader in the different parts of Flanders's witchy realm.

In "The Witch in the Dunes," we meet De Roesschaert. According to the original folktale, she was a witch who lived a secluded life in her cottage. It was a place the locals avoided, and if they did have to be anywhere near her dwelling, they prayed and made the sign of the cross to ward off the evil that lingered in the air. During the time these folktales were collected, Belgium was still a very Catholic country, and you will notice throughout the book that the Catholic faith was often used by the people to protect themselves against beings they considered evil and demonic. One terrible night, De Roesschaert's cottage was destroyed by a storm, and the locals rejoiced. De Roesschaert chooses revenge. She shapeshifts into several animals, including a donkey and a dog in some versions, and sinks vessels. The small community abhors her as she quickly becomes the terror of this small community, but when the sailors baptize themselves for a second time in seawater and take new names, the witch is no longer able to find them and disappears. In the original version, there's no sympathy for the witch, which is the case for most witches, but one does have to wonder here if the villagers are entirely blameless. They, after all, celebrated the loss of her cottage, the only thing that was dear to her. In other versions of this tale, De Roesschaert isn't a witch but a devil, and there are yet other versions in which she is a ghost. Sefa Bubbels is another witch whom the villagers harass, although the villagers might be of the opinion that it was the other way around. The decision was made here to stand with Sefa and her owls, recognizing that shunned witches deserve a voice too, and let's be honest, it's much more fun to align with the witch. Sefa comes from the small village of Beselare in West Flanders, near Ypres, where there's a witches' parade every two years to celebrate the town's witchy past. If the folktales are to be believed, this village once teemed with witches. There aren't many tales in Flanders in which witches have a familiar, but there is an abundance of tales in which witches have the ability to shapeshift into animals. This is very clear in the tale of "Die Gnydige," where cats were their animal of choice. There aren't many witches who choose to take the shape of a toad. This story comes from the only English-language source* that has inspired a retelling in this book. In the original version, Henderson writes that he does not know of "any other instance in which the witch assumes this loathsome shape." This is a sentiment that doubtlessly many will disagree with. In my own humble opinion, toads are the prettiest beings to walk this earth. It says a lot about Flanders that we have one of the very few tales in which a witch chooses to be a toad. It not only confirms our rich storytelling traditions but also the wonderfully dark imaginations of the people who lived here before us. And, of course, their deep-seated fear of witches. Once more, the question that arises here is: which is worse? Preventing a boat from moving forward or stabbing a toad? "The Witch Must Die" is a tale that has many variants. In most of these, the daughter reluctantly accepts her inheritance and is very glad when the priest later rids her of the curse her mother has bestowed upon her. However, in some versions, the daughter sees a new, magical world and simply tells the priest to "go away." Because seeing these stories in a new light and having empathy for the women who were rejected by society is important for this book, the last version is also the version that inspired the reimagined tale here. "Hedges and Bushes" is a spell that is often used by witches to fly to gatherings, and as we'll see later, bokkenrijders often spoke the same words. In lots of folktales, a witch will rub herself with a flying ointment and then speak the spell. Often, someone else wants to follow the witch but gets the words wrong and says "through" instead of "over," resulting in a hellish and painful ride. This tale was inspired by a version about a group of witches, cats, and ghosts who feast together but are disturbed when they realize someone is spying on them. They say to the onlooker, "through hedges and bushes" before they disappear into thin air, and the onlooker endures a torturous voyage as punishment for spying.

Because so many witches live in Flanders, this is also not the last chapter in which they will make an appearance. A lot of these tales overlap, and it would be a shame to let them hide away in their cottages so soon.

* William Henderson, Notes on the folk-lore of the northern counties of England and the borders, 1879.

Creatures of the Woods

THE MAGPIE TREE

Magpies, do you see me? Or am I just as invisible to you as I am in the house of my father and mother? Do you notice the tears rolling down my cheeks? Do you hear the quiver in my voice? Because I see you. Hundreds of you are sitting on the leafless, thick branches of an oak tree, your sleek blue and glossy green feathers glittering only on the spots where the sun can touch them. And I imagine, I imagine your dark acorn-colored eyes watching me.

My father told me to stay away from you. Once, he had to walk through the woods on a moonless night. He said a cat was following him, a cat that wasn't anything at all like our ginger Tom who curls up in front of the fire at home, but a black one with a mean streak in its eyes. Eyes that were said to have the same color as bright blue thistles. Suddenly, the cat disappeared, but something much worse appeared in its place.

Countless magpies flew over his head and landed on the same tree I am looking at now. My father ran as fast as he could. He was certain his eyes would be pecked out, and his skin scratched away by sharp claws if he had walked past that tree.

My mother told me to stay away from you. The unearthly music that you make once woke her up in the middle of the night. She heard your chants and the sound of bare feet dancing on the muddy ground. She heard your evil voices casting a spell that sent a screeching wind blowing through her hair, and she felt your fiery claws shredding her hands and scorching her skin.

The hunter told me to stay away from you. It was a cold autumn day when he saw a lone magpie sitting in a tree and shot it. Underneath the tree, he found a finger with a wedding ring still attached to it instead of a bird. He wanted to gather the villagers to search for more body parts that might be hidden in the woods because he was convinced a grisly murder had been committed. But the neighbors told him that a woman was lying in bed injured. She had lost a finger. A witch.

Witches! You're all witches! Each and every one of you! To be avoided, shunned, and rejected by those who know their prayers for not to know them is to be cursed forever. Curse me! Let me fly with you! Teach me! Teach me how to raise storms and how to blow venom that adheres itself to trees. It's said that the venom transforms into spiders when night falls.

Please, let me sing the raspy magpie song with you. Let us flood this town with a deluge that people will still be talking about fifty years later. But not us, we will forget, we will forget everything and chatter endlessly amongst ourselves. Let me fly. Give me feathers. Let me be you. You!

THE HARES AND THE ACCORDION PLAYER

Frans looked at the laborers, seamstresses, and craftsmen gathering in the market square. He had hidden his cart in the woods nearby because he feared what had happened in the previous village might repeat itself. When the townspeople saw a peddler selling combs, small chalkboards, and used scales enter their small town, they threw stones at him. One man had even threatened to set his cart on fire.

This time, Frans wanted to approach the villagers slowly. Perhaps he would play a song on his accordion and show them that he was a trustworthy fellow who would never attack them in their sleep and run off with all their valuables. He had expected to find them in the pub drinking and swearing but not assembled in the market square.

"What do we do?" a man who stood on a bench asked the crowd, "Are we going to let those fiendish hares murder us all?"

"They didn't murder him," a woman said.

"You think you know better, *mevrouw Lieve*? You always think you know better, don't you?"

"He was a pompous fool," she said. "He's heard the stories often enough, but did he listen? No! He went into the woods. And then what does the fool do? Throws a stick at a hare. What did he expect was going to happen? The hares were going to declare him their master and carry him around in a sedan chair?"

"Are you condoning murder?"

"There was no murder. He scared himself to death. We all know he was chased out of the woods by hundreds of hares.

And I say that he shouldn't have been throwing things at them unless his ingenious plan was to scare himself to death."

"I know what you are. You are one of those long-eared beasts. Aren't you *mevrouw Lieve*? In your hare-form, you drink the blood of innocents and curse those who cross you, and he discovered the truth, didn't he? That's why you and your warren of hares murdered him."

"How dare you? How dare you say I'm a witch? How dare you accuse me of…"

Frans had heard enough. He left the market square and went back to the woods. He stared at the trees behind him through one of his hand mirrors. He waited patiently for a shadow to appear, a sign that there was witchery nearby or something that suggested these woods were bedeviled, but nothing happened, and soon, the song of a hawfinch lulled him to sleep.

It was pitch dark when Frans opened his eyes. He went deeper into the woods. He held his breath when he noticed that his breathing sounded louder than the twigs that creaked beneath his boots and he shivered when the unearthly call of an owl echoed through the forest.

He froze when he suddenly spotted a hare sitting in front of a tree. Frans felt as if its large brown eyes were trying to read what was inside his mind. He saw mercilessness in its eyes, mercilessness towards those who wanted to harm the hare, but also fear, fear of those who wanted to shoot bullets into the animal's heart.

Frans bowed, then opened his knapsack and showed the hare his red accordion. The hare nodded. He strapped the instrument to his chest and pressed the buttons. A tune that sounded more wondrous than anything he had ever played before reverberated through the woods. It didn't take long for another hare to arrive. The two hares stood up, touched each other's paws, and started to dance. Then another hare came, and another, and another, and

just when Frans thought there couldn't be any more hares in the woods, twenty more appeared.

They danced around the trees while he played. As they swirled and twirled, their hind legs ripped the moss out of the earth and created the kind of circles that Frans had often heard others call witches' circles. It was said these circles were cursed, and anyone who stepped into them would be lost forever. But that's not how Frans saw them. As far as he was concerned, the true meaning of the circles was belonging.

Every now and then, a hare would stop dancing and gaze at the moon. When its silver light started to vanish, so did the hares. And that's when Frans started to reevaluate his life. People didn't accept him for who he was, but the hares did. He didn't know if they were shapeshifting witches, but he didn't mind if they were. He belonged in their witches' circle.

Frans soon got to work and built himself a small hut in the woods. It lacked even the most basic of luxuries, and many would declare the crude structure uninhabitable, but Frans didn't care. He had finally learned how to smile. He lived off the bounty the forest had to offer, and sometimes, the hares left bread or cheese at his door. Every night, he played his accordion for the hares as they danced until the sun put an end to the merriness. But it was never truly the end. The moon always returned along with the hares.

THE ENCHANTED RABBITS

Three of us slept in the woods. We had formed a perfect circle; our short, fluffy tails touched each other's backs, and our hind legs swirled into a complex web, but our sleep didn't remain peaceful for long. A man passed by and woke us up. Domesticated rabbits who don't mind being locked up in small cages with the knowledge they would get a carrot and some cabbage in exchange for their freedom might have been content, but we aren't those kinds of rabbits.

We tried to run away from that man, far, far away, but our eyes were sleepy, and he was too quick. He picked us up by our scruffs, put us into a straw basket, and fastened the lid. We didn't mind the darkness inside, but we did mind being shaken around as he walked. When he finally stood still, we were all suffering from terrible stomach aches. After what seemed like an eternity, the man opened the basket and released us into a small wooden shed.

"You'll be happy here," he said, "You're protected from the harsh winter that is bound to come soon, and there are no foxes to be afraid of here either. My bloodhound will keep an eye on you all." He made each of us a bed of hay and then locked the door behind him.

The shed was dreadful. We were surrounded by mooing cows with clouds of flies that buzzed around their hides and rested in the corners of their tired, sore-looking eyes. They sang sad songs inaudible to the human ear, but their dismal tunes lingered in our long ears.

The shed windows were covered in cobwebs and dust, and there was very little room to hop around. The hours passed slowly. We missed the sounds of the forest, the leaves rustling in the wind, the call of woodpeckers, nuthatches, woodlarks, the squirrels scraping holes in the earth to bury their treasures, and especially the howls of passing wolves.

When midnight arrived, we did what we always did when we were in the forest. We shapeshifted into our human forms. I have long gray hair that usually shines under the silver strands of the moon, but there was no light in the shed, and tonight, my hair didn't sparkle. One of my companions had fiery red eyes in which stories of old could be read, along with the power to start fires simply by staring at a bundle of wood. My other companion joined our shapeshifting witches' coven two years ago. He was once a wizard who was cast out by society and decided to become a rabbit until the day his body finally decides to bid this earth farewell.

My companions and I danced around the stacks of hay in the shed and encouraged the cows to join our circle. Yes, we made a lot of noise, but there's nothing delightful in silent balls. I was about to climb on one of the cows and pretend to ride it through the gates of hell when the man who had stolen us entered the shed. He gawped at us as if he was beholding a spectacle so ugly and foul that it wouldn't have appeared in his darkest nightmares.

We had hoped the man might set us free. Who wants two dancing witches and a wizard on their property? But no, he ran screaming out of the shed and bolted the doors behind him.

"He'll soon regret staring at us with such contempt," I said to the others, "free or not free, we shall have our revenge."

When the night made room for the day, we changed back into rabbits and slept. But ere long, the man interrupted us once again. He picked us up by the scruff with even more savageness than he had done the day before and threw us in the basket. We were nauseous from the violent shaking, but most of all, we were worried. We feared he might kill us, and we made plans to jump in his face as soon as he opened the lid and skin him alive.

After a while, the man put the basket down again, and as soon as the lid was opened, we saw that we were back in the woods, at the exact same place from where he had stolen us. The place where we were at our most powerful.

An old magic lingered in these woods that didn't take kindly to humans, and we were ready to scratch this human's eyes out. But then we saw that he was carrying a small bundle in his arms.

"You're lucky," I said to the man, "if you hadn't taken a baby with you, we would have broken your neck."

"You're repulsive," he said, "repulsive!"

"Why steal us when we're so repulsive, eh? Why do it?"

"Oh, trust me, if I had known I had taken dark sorcery into my home, I would have shot the lot of you."

"For this, you will have bad luck until the day you die."

The man laughed and walked away, "bad luck," he murmured, "bad luck? Who do they think they are? The devil himself?"

When we danced in the woods that night, the man's cows joined us. They had broken free and no longer sang sad songs. Soon, the chickens and the man's beloved bloodhound added to our number and stayed with us permanently in the forest. The man's daughter alone consoled him and kept the loneliness that loomed over him like a dark cloud at bay. But when his child grew up, she saw her father's true colors and became a witch herself. She joined us in the forest, leaving the man all by himself. He soon died of grief alone and forgotten.

The Skin of the Wolf

"Jaap told me that our son is a wolf, and I slapped him," I said as I rearranged the cushions in the rocking chair and sat down. "What did that fool expect? I might be old and brittle, scrawny and clumsy, and more interested in books than 'real life,' as our neighbor so often likes to point out, but nobody is going to call my son a wolf."

"Don't you think it's odd that our son always sneaks out of the house when there's a full moon?" my wife asked as she placed a plate of crumpets on the table and poured green tea into cups.

"Surely, you're not on Jaap's side, are you? Has he returned the ladle he borrowed from you? I don't think so, and I guess I won't see my rake back either."

"How about this?" she walked to the window and looked at the dark, thick clouds gathering in the distance, "we follow our son tonight and…"

"We will do no such thing."

"Let me finish," she furrowed her brow, "we follow our son tonight, and in the morning, you can knock on Jaap's door and prove him wrong. Then you can tell him that you have seen with your own eyes that our son isn't a wolf."

"You're saying that I can teach our neighbor a lesson if I sacrifice one night of sleep? Very well, then."

My wife nodded and walked to the kitchen.

I picked up Virginie Loveling's *Een revolverschot* and started to read. But instead of losing myself in a conflict between two sisters and the love they share for the same man, I found myself being pulled back to this world by the racket my wife made in the kitchen as she scrubbed the pots and pans. I tried to focus on the comforting sound of my son sawing wood in the shed but to no avail. He was a clever lad. He often made wooden toys for the children in the village and was now working on a birdhouse for the garden. I picked up the novel again, knowing that I would have to reread the pages as my mind was elsewhere as it often was. Once my thoughts drifted, I could never quite remember what they were like while I was in that world.

"It's time," my wife's voice dragged me back to our dimly lit dining room. I took the oil lamp from the dresser and followed her outside.

"Leave that here," she said, "he'll see us."

"You want us to trip over a fallen tree trunk and die?"

"Look at the moon. It's bright and will be our guide. Come on."

I clasped her hand as we strolled towards an army of skeleton trees. I had never been fond of winter. It seemed as if the world stopped revolving around the sun, and the passage of time had become merely an illusion. I longed for the birds, frogs, and insects to return. I always took them for granted during the summer months and missed them sorely when the landscape turned white.

"Faster, we're losing him," my wife whispered as we entered the woods. She was right about the moon. The trees were so bare that its silver light lit up the forest ground.

"Look," she said. My son had removed a furry skin from a hollow tree and draped it across his shoulders. He sat down on the ground with his head between his knees and howled, causing the trees to tremble. We watched as the skin attached itself to his body, and my son was no longer my son. My eyes grew watery when I saw a gray wolf with a broad snout, pointed ears, and a bushy tail standing in the place where my dear boy had just been. The wolf howled again and disappeared into the darkness.

"I told you he was a wolf!"

My wife and I were startled. Jaap was standing behind us.

"You've got a lot of nerve following us," my hands reached for Jaap's throat, but my wife stepped between us. I knew what happened to werewolves when people found out about them. Hunters chased them through the woods and shot them dead.

"You have two options," said Jaap, "you can shout at me for the whole night, or you can listen to what I have to say and save your son."

"We'll do anything," my wife said.

***

The next morning, our son ate breakfast with us as if nothing had happened. He rubbed his eyes, then went off to the shed. My wife, Jaap, and I snuck out of the house and into the forest. We were relieved to find the skin in the exact same place and hid it in Jaap's house. Then, there was nothing to do but wait. I opened several of my books only to close them seconds later. The hours passed slowly. Would I have my boy back this evening?

As darkness fell, the smoky smell of a bonfire entered our house. My wife and I waited until our son closed the door behind him before we went to Jaap's garden. We tossed the flea-ridden skin into the fire and were astonished when my son appeared in an instant. He was there so quickly it seemed he had flown to Jaap's garden. He screamed. He jumped furiously on the ground and pulled hanks of hair out of his head. My wife tried to stop him when he started to bang his head against Jaap's brick house until his forehead was bloodied, but my neighbor told her to stay where she was. When the skin was nearly burnt up, he sprinted towards me and placed his hands around my neck. He started to strangle me. Jaap attempted to pull my son away from me, but as long as he had wolf's blood running through his veins, he was too strong for us ordinary humans.

I was certain I was going to die, and I had so many thoughts I wanted to be my last that I could not think of anything to think of. Then, all of a sudden, he released me. The fire had completely consumed the furry skin, and a smile appeared on my boy's face. The sickly gray color that had stained his cheeks for several months had now disappeared.

"I'm so sorry," he said, "I didn't want to be a wolf, but I was

63

bitten by one and forced to howl whenever there was a full moon. Now that my wolf skin has been destroyed, I am free and no longer have to roam the woods in the company of all that is malicious."

My son was my son again. He explained that he had never bitten or killed anyone, but he had often forced people to carry him. Jaap wasn't the fool that I thought he was, but there was something that still bothered me.

"How did you know how to save my son?" I asked him one glorious spring morning.

"My nephew was a wolf too," he said, "we had to travel far and wide to find out how to break the curse, and it was all for nothing. They shot him. I didn't want you to go through what I have been through."

From that day forward, Jaap was allowed to borrow and not return things as often as he liked. I had my son, and that was all that mattered. He was safe and sound, making wooden dolls and horses for the children to play with, and he never looked at the moon or went into the woods again.

JAKKO

"Is this how it ends?" he asked as Sara tucked him underneath another blanket, "I'm not even worthy of a farewell?"

"I'm sure he'll be here soon, father."

"My own flesh and blood would rather go hunting than hear the last words his father will ever speak."

"I'm your child too, and I'm here," she gave him another spoon of laudanum.

"I'm sick, not blind," his skeletal hands gripped the bedside table, knocking the framed picture of Sara's long-deceased mother onto the worn wooden floor.

Sara sat on the edge of the bed, staring at the broken glass. She thought she could see her mother's spirit rising into the air as she departed the glass cage. The cage where she had imprisoned herself to protect the man she had left behind in the knowledge that his time to follow her had come. For a moment, she even thought she could hear her mother ripping fabric in two as she often did before sewing a dress. But it was her father tearing the bed curtains from the rods as he stumbled out of the room.

"Stay in bed, please," she cried, "he will come; I know he will come."

"I've never known you to be a liar," her father said. His breathing was labored as he descended the stairs. Sara followed. She implored him to go back to bed, but he ignored her in the same way he had when she was four. She wanted to give him a daisy she had plucked in the fields. It was her earliest memory and one she often thought of when he continued to ignore her throughout the years.

"Where are you?" her father opened the front door and invited the biting wind into the hallway. Sara thought he had wanted to shout, but his hoarse voice sounded like a whisper.

"What have I ever done to you, Jakko?" Her father's scrawny knees stuck out from his nightdress as he stepped over the threshold. "Well…curse you then! I curse you! You are no son of mine! May you hunt forever if hunting animals in the woods is more important than visiting your old man on his deathbed. Forever, I say!"

Sara heard a high-pitched scream coming from the woods. It was the kind of scream that would make ancient oak trees shudder and lose their leaves out of sheer fright. She didn't dare to think of the countless terrifying occurrences those trees must have witnessed in their lifetimes, but a little voice in her head whispered that the worst was yet to come. She briefly imagined that she'd long ago left her father's house, moved to the city, and was surrounded by people who cared. People who would wipe away her tears on lonely nights, but now it was too late. There was no time. Her father had collapsed.

Sara tried to shake him awake, though she knew he was gone. She continued to slap him softly on the cheek, hoping to bring him back to life. It was no use.

She lifted her father from the stone entrance upon which he had fallen and placed his head in her lap. She stroked his hair while tears trickled down her cheeks and splashed into his eyes. She thought how strange it was that her father had once cried in the crib to announce to the world that he was a living, breathing being. Perhaps it was the only time in his life he had ever cried. Sara could now, with certainty, say that her father would never cry again.

When she stood up, she was surprised to see her blue skirt was drenched with blood. She wondered if her father's illness was the cause of his death or if her brother had killed him.

Her brother wasn't at her father's funeral. That didn't surprise Sara since she often had to remind herself what her sibling even looked like. She remembered the time Jakko had paraded a deer's head on a cart while her father had complained about the pain in his back and asked his son to help reap the crops. Her brother said that her father should eat the deer meat. He claimed that it would heal his father's ailments, and then he could do the work himself. It didn't work. Sara's brother only came to the farm when his clothes needed mending or his boots needed cleaning. Once, she watched him sing as he skinned a rabbit, giggling as he forcefully tore the fur off the rabbit. She had always thought her brother was a brute.

After the funeral, she returned to an empty home. It was quiet. Too quiet. That night, the screeching of a bird interrupted her dreams. She could hear her brother's name in those screeches. Jakko. She blamed it on her lively imagination as she drifted into a dream. The farm belonged to her now. She would prove that she was just as good a farmer as her brother would have been if he had never entered those woods.

Her dream turned into a real-life nightmare when death arrived at her doorstep the following morning in the shape of a dead chicken. The next day, it was a dead fox, but nothing could have prepared her for what she would find on the windowsill on the third day: an arm. It was ripped off from the shoulder, bruised and discolored, with a rose-colored bracelet still adorning the wrist.

Sara didn't go to bed that night. She sat on the doorstep with a cup of tea while she listened to the rain and stared at the pitch-black forest that lay behind the fields. Every now and then, she heard the snapping of twigs being flattened by hedgehogs and the growls of wild boars in the distance. Then came the sound she had been waiting for, the spine-tingling cry of a bird who screamed Jakko!

Jakko! Jakko! Jakko! A hawk flew toward her. She raised her arms to protect her head and cried out in horror when the hawk's curved talons left deep cuts across her arms. The bird flew back into the starless night and disappeared. Sara shouted in fright when the hawk returned and tore at her cheek.

"You're Jakko, my brother," Sara yelled as the hawk disappeared again, "I undo father's curse! Devouring beasts and men in the woods for all eternity isn't a fate that should be yours. I dislike you with a vengeance, but come back to me, brother, come back, Jakko!"

The hawk swooped down one final time. Its knife-like talons punctured Sara's neck and ended her life. *Jakko! Jakko! Jakko!* The hawk screeched in triumph. There could be no life where Jakko was. He hated it. Life.

THE HAUNTED FOREST

On a tree is written: His name was Isidoor. He was a forester.

There was something wrong with the forest. Isidoor placed his hand on one of the beech trees. He had only been a forester for two weeks, but even city rats who played cards in the pub while nearly suffocating on their own pipe smoke knew that trees weren't supposed to wake you up in the middle of the night. Trees weren't supposed to scream.

Isidoor lay his hand on the uneven bark of another tree. He looked up at the stars. Aside from the screaming trees, the forest was too quiet. No mice rustled through the leaves, no owls hooted, and no crickets chirped. A sharp pain stabbed Isidoor's hand. He jerked away from the tree, sensing that the tree had been moving its feelings into his body. Wretchedness and despair. Loneliness and hatred, a hatred so intense that Isidoor could not imagine anyone feeling that way, let alone a tree.

He walked deeper into the woods and was careful not to touch any of the trees. He feared they would fill his soul with so much anguish that he would no longer be in control of his body. Was he going mad? Should he tell someone? Would they lock him up in an asylum if he did? Would they confine him to an empty, windowless room? Would they chain him to the walls in order to force his madness to leave? There was only one thing that he could do. Ignore what he had seen, felt, and heard. Trees don't have any feelings, and they certainly cannot scream.

He wanted to prove to himself that he was merely dreaming. He broke off the branch of a tree. It cried out. A liquid dropped on the ground from the cracked branch. Could it be? No.

Impossible. It was too dark to see the color, but he touched it with his finger and placed it on his tongue. Blood. Yes, it was blood. There was no mistaking the iron taste of blood. The tree screamed again. Isidoor covered his ears and started to run. He was going to return to his cottage, bolt the doors, and remain there until daylight broke. He ran as fast as he could, but as he zigzagged between the trees, it didn't feel like he would reach his cottage quickly enough.

Isidoor saw something in the distance that wasn't a tree. A shadow? A ghost? A presence that should not exist? He couldn't work out what the foggy figure floating towards him was. What he could see was that it had hands, hands that were reaching for his throat. The figure started to strangle him, and its sharp fingernails entered his neck. Everything around Isidoor grew hazy, and he knew he would soon be unconscious. Part of him wanted to fight, and another part wanted to embrace whatever would come after this life.

"Oi, you! Let him go!" Someone shouted.

"I will make victims," the figure withdrew and floated back into the distant darkness, but the words echoed throughout the forest. *I will make victims.*

"Are you alright?"

"Who are you?" Isidoor asked as he gasped for breath. He estimated that the man who had driven his would-be murderer away was around thirty years of age, though he couldn't tell for sure because a beard hid the man's chin.

"Come with me," the man said, "you need a cup of tea and perhaps a slice of apple cake."

Isidoor followed the stranger. They left the dense woods behind them and walked along the path. He had never liked paths, but he was happy to walk on one now. He changed his mind when he saw what they were walking toward. He had heard of the castle that nobody dared to enter. It was said to be a place where death ruled. The man who had laid the first brick died centuries ago, and death had never left the castle grounds since.

Isidoor wanted to return to his cottage, but he didn't want to walk back through the haunted forest again, nor did he want to be rude to his savior. Yet, at the same time, he didn't really want to admit that he had ever been in danger. That would mean ghosts were real, and they weren't.

The man smiled when he saw Isidoor's shaking hands, "it's

quite alright," he said, "nothing's going to happen here tonight that wouldn't have happened at your cottage." He opened the door and led Isidoor into a room. A coat of arms hung over a fireplace depicting two bears hugging. A portrait of a woman hung above it. She wore a 17th-century headdress and clasped a rose in her hands. On the other side of the room, there was a portrait of a man. Isidoor thought he had seen this man before, but it wasn't possible. Where would he have met a man with so much hatred in his eyes that he would make even the most cheerful being on this planet wish they ceased to exist when glimpsing his face?

"I must apologize for that encounter in the woods," the man said.

"Why?" Isidoor asked, "I think we're finding ourselves in a nightmare, and besides, you weren't the one trying to strangle me, were you?"

"No," he said while he poured out tea, "but the same blood that runs through his veins runs through mine. Well…I'm not sure about that. He's been dead for a long time, and I have no idea if ghosts have veins or not."

"What about those…those trees?"

"You truly didn't know what you were getting yourself into when you accepted to be employed here, did you?" he raised an eyebrow, "there are more ghosts than living things in those woods. My ancestors made sure of that. They excelled at breeding and dying. I've heard that the priests banished them to trees, forcing them to remain there for a hundred years, and that's why the trees scream. They're trapped ghosts."

"You think I believe that?" Isidoor jumped out of his armchair. "You think I'm that mad?"

"If you don't believe in ghosts after everything that happened tonight, then you are mad," the man said, "there's a lady who…" He stopped speaking when there was a knock at the door. Another knock followed. And then another, and then a bang. A bang filled with rage, fury, and hatred. It was the ghost.

"I was a sinner once, and now I ensure sinners are punished, and justice is served," the voice sounded just as loud as if it had been standing next to them, "I will make victims."

Isidoor paced back and forth as the room grew colder. He told himself that he would soon wake up and not remember anything of that night. That's what would happen. But if it was a nightmare, why did the fear and terror feel so real?

"You better have some brandy," the stranger said as he opened a bottle, "it will be your last."

"Sins…" Isidoor said, "it wants to punish those who have been sinful. I'm not wrathful or envious. I'm not a proud man, and I don't care about material goods. I'm not consumed with desire for anyone or anything, and I'm not idle. I very much doubt sandwiches with jam are gluttonous. I don't have any sins."

"Are you sure about that?" the man asked, "are you really, really sure?"

Isidoor didn't answer. He drained the glass of brandy and poured himself another one.

***

My name is Isidoor. I was a forester until a ghost murdered me. I'm now a tree in the woods that screams when night falls. It's a horrendous and insufferable fate, but one day, I will walk again, and when I do, I will punish the sinful. I will make victims.

ENDNOTES

Enchanted woods and magical forests are something all of us occasionally dream of. We often imagine them as fairy lands with mystical rays of sunlight shining through and inhabited by whimsical and often mischievous creatures. For the most part, this does not apply to Flanders, and not only due to the absence of fairies in our storytelling traditions. The woods here are dangerous. It's where witches, ghosts, and ravenous beasts dwell, and the magic that swirls around the trees is dark magic. "The Magpie Tree" is inspired by the belief that witches can shapeshift into magpies and combines three folktales that were once told in these lands. Each time the narrator says, "My…told me to stay away from you," we have a new folktale. The "Hares and the Accordion Player" combines two folktales. The first story tells of a man who threw a stick at a hare and would soon regret it. He was chased by hundreds of hares out of the forest and died not long after. The moral that animals should never be harmed is one we rightfully often see in Flemish folktales. The second story is about an accordion player who was said to have a devilish streak and played music for the hares. As hares were often believed to be shapeshifting witches, there are references to this in the reimaging too. In "The Enchanted Rabbits," we once again meet a group of shapeshifters. While the original folktale strongly implies that these rabbits are pure evil, it is interesting to note that they refuse to attack the man who stole them away from the forest because he's holding a baby. In other versions, animals that are taken home by people often transform into stones and skulls and must be carried back to the spot from where they were seized. "In The Skin of the Wolf," we meet one of the many werewolves that roam Flanders. The version included here is one that was frequently told in Flanders. In most stories, the werewolves are reluctant werewolves and desperately want someone to undo the curse. Most Flemish werewolves will not slaughter whole villages but will force people to carry them. We haven't met Kludde yet, but it is interesting to note that Kludde, on whom there will be much more later, also forces people to carry him. While Jakko doesn't murder his sister in the original folktale, and lots of mystery surrounds him as we're not even sure what bird species he belonged to, we do know that he was the nightmare of the forest and devoured beasts and men alike. The dying father cursing his son because he didn't bid his father farewell also reminds one of "The Seven Ravens" and other fairytales in which parents inadvertently curse their children into changing into animals. However, in Jakko's case, nobody undoes the curse. And because he's obsessed with hunting, he can't stop hunting in his bird shape either, and quickly becomes one of the most murderous creatures to live in the woods. In "The Haunted Forest," we also discover how frightening these woods can be, and let's hope that none of us ever encounters Isidoor. The clergy often banished ghosts and evil spirits to trees in which they were forced to live for one hundred years or until the tree died. If the folktales are to be believed, this resulted in some forests being the most haunted places in Flanders which nobody dared to enter.

DEVILS

THE BLUE BARN

"I need another barn, and the devil may build it for all I care. I must have another barn," Joost said as he stared at the bundles of sheaves piled so high they were doomed to rot. The farmhand had stacked them in front of the timber barn Joost's grandfather had built. The old fool never thought that maybe one summer, there would be enough sunshine for a good harvest. The upcoming weeks were bound to bring rainfall, and Joost would have to watch how all the grain he had harvested became soaked. He could already see weevils, mice, and rats thriving on his misfortune.

As Joost took a swig from the jenever bottle he kept hidden inside his useless barn, he spotted a tall man approaching from the gates. The stranger wore a dinner jacket and top hat as he traveled up the gravel path that brought customers to the farmhouse. The man's ornately carved carriage, pulled by four magnificent black horses, stood waiting by the gates.

"What do you want?" Joost asked as he snuck a look around him. He was relieved to see his wife wasn't anywhere near, as she would frequently scold him for the brusque manner he used on customers. But he was a farmer, not an accordion player entertaining the masses.

"Eggs," the man said.

"Eggs?" Joost scratched his head. Why would a man who looked as if he was searching for his private opera box in *La Monnaie* want eggs?

The stranger nodded and pointed at the towering piles of sheaves. "I see there is no room left in your barn."

"We've got plenty stored, *Monsieur*. The majority will be sold on the markets, but if your household needs grain, we're happy to help out. We also sell apples from our orchard and…"

"And what will you do with those sheaves? Throw them all away?"

"Look, *Monsieur*, how many eggs did you say you want?"

"What if I help you?" the man asked, rubbing his hands together. What if I told you that I could build you a new barn in a single night?"

"With all due respect, *Monsieur*, what if I told you I could walk on walls and pluck the moon out of the sky?"

"I won't be needing the moon," he laughed, "all I need in exchange is your soul."

"Ha! If there's a barn here tomorrow, then my soul is yours."

"It will be finished before the rooster crows," the stranger said as he strolled back to his carriage.

Fool, Joost thought, *even forgot his eggs*. He poured some jenever into a glass as a lackey opened the carriage door for the stranger. The glass tumbled out of his hands, leaving splashes of jenever and tiny glass shards embedded in his mucky shoes when Joost saw that the carriage didn't ride away but flew off the ground and vanished into thin air. He realized he had just made a pact with the devil. He wanted to scream and beg the evil stranger to return and undo the cursed deal he had just made, but he knew it was too late.

Joost fed the chickens with the stale bread his wife had soaked in a cup of water, drove the cattle into a different paddock, and took one last look at the sheaves, this time wishing that vermin would claim it as their own. He entered the farmhouse and climbed the stairs to the bedroom, where he could already hear his wife snoring.

He staggered to the window, brooding over the fate of his poor soul. Through the panes of glass, he watched in horror as the devil erected four huge walls with the same ease as Joost had placed sugar cubes on top of each other this morning while he waited for the kettle to boil. The devil opened a can of paint and with his evil hands began to paint the barn blue. As he painted, the devil's long legs danced to a silent tune; all Joost could hear was the roar of the devil's laughter.

"Wake up," Joost shook his wife's arm, and she opened her eyes. Despite her habitual snoring, she was a light sleeper.

"Whatever's the matter?" she asked.

Joost's hands were shaking as he told her about the devil. His wife tried to interrupt him several times as he monologued about how he would soon no longer have a soul. What was he going to do without a soul? The spirit that made him a living, breathing man? Would the dedication he had shown for his farm now go to spreading evil? Torturing sinners? Drowning children in the nearby river? The thought was unbearable, and he buried his head under the pillows.

"You, idiot!" Joost's wife shouted at him as she stormed to the window.

Joost followed his wife and peeked through the glass. His heart sank when he saw that the devil had almost finished the roof. His wife sighed, then clapped her hands loudly once, twice, three times, and finally a fourth. Suddenly, Joost heard the familiar sound that woke him up every morning, though it was nowhere near the time when sunlight touched the earth yet.

COCK-A-DOODLE-DOO!

The devil's eyes narrowed, his face turned bright red, and steam shot out of his ears.

"There will be no soul-snatching today," Joost's wife shouted at the devil, "the rooster is awake, and you haven't yet finished the barn!"

The devil shouted as he violently slammed his fist into the ground. The barn flew apart like a house of cards. All that was left was a deep gaping hole from which the sound of tortured screams could be heard. The void was so vast that no matter how hard they tried, it was impossible to fill. Soon, the farmer and his wife found themselves out on the streets. Their beloved farm was no longer their home but was now the permanent haunt of unearthly creatures who screeched and wailed in the night.

The Ship's Log

Thursday, 16th of May, 1889

9:00 PM First entry due to unforeseen circumstances. A
moderate breeze with a wind speed of an estimated 12.2 knots.
If conditions remain favorable as we cross the Atlantic, we are
on track to reach Philadelphia on the 23rd of May. I've
witnessed many strange things on many long voyages, but this
day upon this ship betrays all my good sense and reason. This
morning, the crew woke with a lively, rosy color in their cheeks
that quickly faded as the day progressed.

The captain was nowhere to be found, but it was his habit to
show up before long. What concerned me was reports of a shrill,
disembodied laugh coming from the hold. Though it was most
likely a stowaway, two men were sent to investigate while I
took the helm.

As the day waned, the crew became pale and still like
skeletons. Investigation of their rapid deterioration led back to
the hold from which our two men had never returned. My own
inspection of the room revealed our textile cargo was still
perfectly intact. Bloody footprints, reminiscent of a beast, with
no clear sign of their origin, marked the floors and walls. In the
blackest corner, I saw what can only be described as two hands
with long, sharp claws digging inside a crate of lace and tossing
the fabric into the air. This was not possible. The sea deceives
mine eyes with a trick of shadow flickering in dim light. I exited
and slammed the hold's door shut.

Friday, 17th of May 1889

9:15 AM First entry. A moderate breeze with an estimated wind speed of 13.00 knots. As far as I'm aware, The captain is not in his cabin nor anywhere on the ship, and our two crewmen are still missing. The eighteen passengers who are traveling with us have noticed something is not as it should be and are growing restless. I told them the captain suffered from a headache and ordered an extra portion of buttered biscuits for everyone as an apology for his absence. I assured them that the captain would soon return. This seemed to alleviate their concerns.

14:16 AM Second entry. A moderate breeze with an estimated wind speed of 14.06 knots. The shrill laugh can still be heard in the ship's hold, but by now, it is no longer the only concerning sound aboard. Several passengers and crew have reported hearing echoing sounds of horses neighing and whinnying over the crash of the waves. The sea has often deceived me, but I'm not sure it has the power to deceive so many ears all at once.

10:45 PM Third entry. A storm force of an estimated 60.8 knots. The ship is surrounded by waves mightier than those of Poseidon or any God who lives in treacherous seawater. Our fate would be better if the ship sank and what happened here became an unexplained sea mystery, but alas, at the time of this writing, some sort of dark magic protects us and keeps us from harm. It is most unnatural. The deck should be drenched with water, but not a drop has fallen on the wooden planks. The thunder should be deafening, but it is so quiet that I can hear the ship's cat purring and the crew whispering about the dark forces at work here. The mast should be wobbling. No, not wobbling; it should have cracked by now. We should be saying our last prayers and confessing our sins, but everything remains eerily still. The misty curtain that protects us from doom must be feared. The passengers continue to discuss the possibility of restless spirits dwelling in that veil of mist, with some saying that doomed souls will pull us into an evil world where we will be cursed to wander eternally in a desert filled with whalebones.

11:13 P.M. Fourth entry. A storm of an estimated 62.6 knots still rages around the ship without doing any harm. The captain suddenly appeared out of nowhere. His eyes were now a reddish yellow instead of the usual blue, with blood dripping from his overgrown, claw-like nails. The surgeon ran to him and asked if he had wounded himself, but the captain angrily pushed him away. He rebuked the crewmembers who had gathered around him and said he was well within his rights to go for a stroll on his own ship without accounting for his whereabouts or strange appearance. The captain said the next man who came near him without his permission would be shot and went to his cabin.

God, be my strength. The captain has gone insane, the passengers are cursing themselves for having booked passage on a cargo ship instead of an ocean liner, and the word 'mutiny' is whispered amongst the crew. I asked the barrelman if there was another ship nearby, and he said it was beyond the realm of possibility. And even if there was such a hapless ship, the sea was too hungry for it to remain afloat amid these wicked waves.

11:55 PM Fifth entry. A storm of an estimated…oh, I no longer have the mind to concern myself with knots. The barrelman pierced the silence from his crow's nest and shouted that he saw something approaching, but it wasn't a ship.

We stared in disbelief as a carriage, drawn by four muscular black horses, rode over the waves. As the carriage landed on deck, one of the horses nearly trampled one of the crewmen to death. A man with a top hat and fancy black overcoat stepped out and introduced himself as a lord. I risked being shot and alerted the captain about the unexpected visitor. The captain just stared at me unfazed and ordered me to bring the lord to him along with a bottle of wine.

12:30 AM Sixth entry. Horrendous noises are coming out of the captain's cabin. There's that shrill laugh again, but it now sounds like it's being throttled. The voice sounds strangely familiar, like the captain, but more maniacal and malignant. I considered whether to open the door or not but as I struggled to make up my mind, everything suddenly went quiet.

An eerie stillness fell over the cabin. It seemed to last for hours but was probably only a few seconds. The lord smashed the door against my nose as he stormed out of the cabin and rode back out to sea in his carriage. I entered the cabin, but the captain wasn't there. I saw what looked like a human ear on his desk. A hand with claw-like nails lay on the shelf beneath the stained glass window, depicting a sailing ship in all its pride and glory. It could only be the captain's hand. Though I covered my nose when I saw a dark-brown wedge-shaped sponge on the floor, I vomited. It was a liver. It wasn't just the sight of ripped-out organs that made the room unbearable to be in, but the air was filled with a stench of torment and agony that could only come from hell. Through the sulphuric fug in the cabin, I spied a letter on the desk.

Ahoy,

As you can see, I have torn your captain into pieces. Don't look so appalled! He begged me to die. Your 'honorable' captain made a deal with me a long time ago. He lived the life he desired, but now his time has expired, and his body and soul belong to me. I ate his left arm, but I don't recommend it. He isn't as tasty as he looks. Perhaps he would have been tastier if sprinkled with more wine and some parsley. Be that as it may, I heartily recommend that you stay away from this cabin and hurry yourselves back to land, or you will all be lost at sea.

Bon voyage, smooth sailing, have a trouble-free journey, and avaunt!

The Devil.

P.S. If any of you desire to make a deal with me, I can be found at a crossroad of your choice every night at midnight except for Sundays.

THE COUNT WHO MARRIED THE DEVIL

I am a spirit who dwells in the air, water, fire, and earth. The wind carries me through the sky to where I want to be. I can sleep in streams and seas, hide underneath the soil, and whisper through the flames. When I was born, they told me I could see everything. It was a lie.

My mind returns wistfully to the blissful days before I knew the awful truth. The Count of Flanders was hunting in the woods. He smiled as a wild boar breathed its last, and though the sight of the dead animal made him cheerful, I did not judge him. He was a good count who desired his people to be as healthy and rich as he was.

It was in those woods that he happened to meet a noble lady. She rode towards him on a palfrey bedecked with black dahlias. Her long brown hair was decorated with small tiny silver stones, and a cherry red moonflower was pinned to her night-blue dress.

"Hoogwelgeboren Vrouwe," the count addressed her, "pardon my impertinence, but may I enquire if you are lost? You are too fine a lady to travel without an escort."

"I come from the faraway land of Morningdew," the lady said in a voice sweeter than that of a nightingale, "I have heard that a valiant count rules these lands. He is said to be nothing like the many unprincipled suitors who have asked for my hand in my country, and I desire to speak with him."

"You're speaking with him," the Count said.

The lady dismounted gracefully and bowed. The count escorted her to his castle, where he held a grand banquet in her

honor. The two shared stories, laughed, and whispered into each other's ears, and though I don't have a mouth or a face, a smile appeared in my heart when I saw them holding hands.

The count had sent his father to an early grave by proclaiming he would be the last of his bloodline and would never wed, but the following morning, he announced that he was engaged. Unfortunately, his father never witnessed that happy day.

Six days later, the wedding bells tolled, and all of Flanders feasted. There were lavish meals even for those who often survived on paltry crumbs on days when the clergy offered alms, and butchers and bakers handed out scraps. The people danced with joy. It was an alliance of divine love that would bring wealth and peace to the county, as everyone knows a happy count rules more wisely than a lonely one.

Then, the storm came. A storm so mighty that it wrecked not only the timber houses where most of the population lived but also the monasteries, cathedrals, and even fortified castles that had persevered while beleaguered by countless enemies. The people slept on the streets with the remnants of their broken chairs, tables, and cupboards, and in fields where the crops had been destroyed or in the ravaged woods where so many trees had died.

Then, there was the famine. The poor died first. Few had grain stored in underground cellars but when the hoards of thieves wielding axes and halberds arrived, death was dealt to all. Many fled to the forest. They hoped to survive on blueberries, brambles, and nuts, but that hope turned to ash when they found the forest empty of edible forage and were reduced to eating grass and tree bark. And there were those I could not bear to think of, the ones who ate the flesh of those who were no longer among us or even their own fingers. So many suffered. So many died. So many resembled skeletons and didn't have the strength to bury the thousands of rotten corpses scattered across the land.

Then, the war came. Masked horsemen who were not of this

world slaughtered all those who still had a pulse. They were rumored to be demons, but many claimed that the horsemen were the souls of those who had died in the famine, an unbearable thought to some who refused to believe that their sons, mothers, daughters, and fathers would kill. As a spirit, I knew the truth. Those who loved you could turn into brutes when their bodies were cold and warmth and kindness could no longer reach them.

The count prayed. He asked God for the killing to stop and refused to leave the chapel as he believed that only the one who had created this earth could save them now. One of his councilors disagreed. He had noticed how the countess continued to wear luxurious dresses and partake in sumptuous meals. He had seen her smile as she cavorted from room to room. He had never seen a tear in her eye and had never heard an exclamation of despair leave her lips.

The councilor suspected there was an evil force at work. He confronted the countess. The words she spoke next murdered my faith in myself.

"I'm wearing the body of a lady who once lived in the land of Morningdew. She was sleeping for all eternity underneath an effigy, alone in the darkness, a dreadful place where her smile, her eyes, and her sweet voice had no power. It was a waste for such a perfect vessel as she was. I resurrected her body, but not her soul. Then, I met the count. He married me, and with my position as a countess, I could use my power to feed off grief, terror, and desperation."

"You haven't answered the question," the councilor said, "who are you?"

"I'm the devil," she fell lifeless to the ground, but everyone in the realm refused to believe that she had truly died. Instead, they wondered whose dead body she was going to steal next to wreak havoc and spread evil upon this world.

That was when I knew I was a lie. A spirit who could see

everything had not seen the devil that lived in the body of the countess, the venom that dwelt in her tongue, or the malevolence that resided in her bones. It was my duty to protect and I had failed.

The guilt-ridden count set off on a pilgrimage to Rome and was never seen again. I crawled into a dark cave. If I could not see everything, I would rather see nothing at all. What is the point of a spirit that protects when it cannot see evil? Patiently, I wait. I wait for death to embrace me. Patiently because we can live for thousands of years—years that will be spent in sorrow for the Flanders I could not save.

Battle for a Soul

The devil laughed.

"You believe a church will keep me away?" the devil blew a fiery breath at the wooden cross that stood on top of the church, reducing it to ash, "is it not a mere structure? A structure that can be burned to the ground?"

The priest ignored the devil and dragged his unconscious brother over the threshold. The devil heard him bolting the doors with great effort and smiled. The priest's brother had been all the villagers could talk about lately. His soul was possessed by thousands of little fiends, and the man no longer knew his own name. He had suffered from convulsions, had difficulty breathing, and his skin had turned yellow as the fiends nibbled on his lungs and liver.

Of course, the priest knew what to do. He reasoned that if the possessed renounced the devil in the house of God, the fiends would be forced to leave his body. The devil chuckled. He knew what the priest wanted to do. While the man of the cloth wasn't technically wrong, he wasn't going to let that happen. The soul of the priest's brother belonged to him, and a church would not save them. You cannot hide from the devil.

Like a ghost, the devil flew through the doors. "There's nothing you can do, priest. His soul is mine."

"You won't have him, not today or any other day," the priest cried out as he laid his brother on the altar. The devil took the form of an enormous black dog and chased the priest. He knocked over medieval statues that depicted the Madonna and Child and Jesus with outstretched hands, seeking to inspire

those who walk past him to have faith in God who dwells in the
heavens. The deafening crash of marble breaking echoed
through the church. The black dog's eyes glowed like fire as the
priest threw chairs at him. The dog jumped on the priest and bit
his face, but the priest managed to wrestle himself free. He
splashed holy water on the devil.

"No amount of holy water will keep me away," the devil said
as he transformed into a hawk.

The battle raged on. The marble pieces the priest threw at the
devil failed to strike the foul being. As the devil flew onto the
altar, he changed back into his abhorrent, true shape and placed
his hand in the chest of the possessed to snatch his soul out of
his body.

The priest ran to the altar and threw himself across his brother.
"Satan, I will give my life before I'll allow you to take my
brother's soul," he said breathlessly, "this soul is mine."

The devil roared. The fact that the priest was willing to
sacrifice himself to save the soul of his brother defeated him.
The devil had lost the battle.

***

But had he truly lost? Was he not the devil? And did he not
require a soul? After the battle, the priest went home and
climbed into bed. While the priest's wounds were attended to by
the best doctors in the province, the thought of the priest
surviving this ordeal repulsed the devil. He crawled through the
window in the shape of thick black smoke and smothered the
priest. He had lost the brother's soul, but by killing his
adversary, the devil had something far more precious: the soul
of a priest.

The Gatekeeper of Hell

I have a story to tell. I don't want to take it to my grave, but I have no desire to tell it while I'm still alive. My neighbors would judge me, and they would tell their sons and daughters. The rumors of what I have done would spread like wildfire. There would be no escape from their disapproving stares. They have every right to despise me, but they will have to wait until I'm dead, which is why I'm writing this letter.

I have a son. His mother died while giving birth. It would have been better if I had been alone, but I met a beautiful woman in the woods. She became my wife and took care of the house while I harvested wood and sold it to barons and castellans. One of the advantages of being a woodcutter is that my family was just as warm during the winter months as those of noble blood. Yet there was no harmony in my home. My boy was never happy. He treated his stepmother with contempt. He smeared mud on clean laundry and placed dead mice and rats into pots and pans. Once, he called her an unsightly fly that he wanted to whack to death.

My wife wasn't a saint either. She often hid my son's clothes so that he would have nothing to wear. She threw plates, cups, and chairs at him and once called him a cockroach that she wanted to squeeze to death.

One of them had to go. How could I live without my wife, who sang me to sleep every evening? Who kissed me and told me everything would be fine when I was feeling low? Who made me laugh when no joke could make me grin? My son had to go.

"You will seek employment. Even if you have to serve the

devil himself, you will seek employment." That's what I said to him. He would leave this house and become a stonemason, or work in an apothecary, or as a bookbinder or a servant. I didn't care what he might do as long as he was gone.

I know what you're thinking, and no, I'm not that cruel. I didn't oust him with a knapsack filled with food to last him two weeks. This isn't a fairytale. No, I went with him. My son and I walked towards Antwerp. The familiar sounds of scurrying foxes, whistling birds, and buzzing insects soon made way for rumbling carriage wheels on unpaved roads. My boy was excited. He had never been to the big city before. We were still walking when night fell, and as we crossed a crossroads, my wish became a reality.

A black carriage engraved with ravens, crows, and those twirly things I can never quite describe stopped. A tall man who had barely any flesh on his bones but was very handsome stepped out of the carriage. He introduced himself as a lord and said he was looking for young, strong boys to work in a palace. I told him it was his lucky night. My son was compliant and never asked questions. He was a hard worker, keen to learn, and reliable. The lord offered him employment for three years, and I accepted in the name of my son.

I could tell he was disappointed that he wouldn't see Antwerp with its cathedral and the grand homes of burghers. He had heard much about the houses that rose up in *trapgevels* and touched the gray sky with stepping stones on the scaled gables that told the stories of the trader's successes. I promised him we would go to Antwerp in three years' time. I hugged him and left.

The birds didn't whistle while I made the journey back home, and I sincerely hoped that my son would be compliant. Obedience had never been his forte while he lived under my roof, but that might be different under the roof of a stranger. It struck me that the lord had never said what the nature of his employment would be. In a palace. That was all I knew. Where was there even a palace? *Palais du Coudenberg* in Brussels had burned down thirty years ago, and surely he didn't mean for my son to work in France? And what was his name? Lord? Lord of what?

I didn't go home but knocked on the church doors. The priest sighed when I told my story. The lord was the devil, he said. I pulled at his chasuble in a state of despair. I begged him to help me, but the priest said there was nothing that could be done.

I went home. My beautiful wife was ill with a fever. She soon died. I had never liked to cry, but in the years that followed, I was so broken-hearted that crying was all I had energy for. I had lost my wife and had rented my son to the devil. The three years passed slowly. I lived alone, bereaved, and with a feeling of unbearable guilt that would never go away. I returned to the crossroads after three years, hoping to see my son again. If I could only hold him one more time and tell him how sorry I am, I might finally be able to look in the mirror again.

And there he was, my son! Standing in the middle of the road with crossed arms. I ran to him. What followed was a conversation I'll never forget.

"Good manners of you to pick me up, father," my boy said, "but you aren't getting a cut from my wages."

"What do you take me for? Give your old man a hug, my boy," but the look in his eyes warned me not to step any closer.

"I've got enough gold to build myself a palace now," he said, opening a wooden box filled with gold coins and gemstones. My boy held a red stone that shone brightly between his fingers, and as he showed it to me, something dreadful happened. It changed into dust.

"You tricked me!" he shouted at the dust on the ground, "you deceiving, swollen-headed miscreant! I'll dig you out. That's what I'll do, and I won't stop digging until I have what you promised me!"

"Easy, my boy," I said, "is this where you worked? Under the ground?"

"I was the gatekeeper."

"To the palace?"

"To hell."

"Hell?"

"In many ways, it was a palace. A palace of horror and torture. I opened the gates for the damned souls who were condemned to suffer for all eternity."

"I'm sorry, my boy. I never meant that you should go and work for the devil. That isn't what I wanted for you at all."

"It's okay, father. Opening the gates for my stepmother cheered me up. She tried to run away, but the fire-spitting gargoyles got her. And the priest is having brain surgery without any anesthetic. The doctors estimate he will be out of surgery in ten thousand years."

My son continued to curse the devil for his useless wages as we walked home. In the years that followed, my boy refused to work anywhere out of fear that they would trick him. I didn't mind. I know that I will go to hell. I kicked my own son out and gave him to the devil. It's why I'm trying so hard not to die— but old age is winning. It won't be long before I am with my beautiful wife again, though I doubt she will have any beauty left.

Before I die, I will visit Antwerp with my son once more. We'll sit on the square at night and imagine that alvermannekes, hard-working gnomes who do the laundry and dishes in exchange for food, climb the *trapgevels* to look at the moon.

The Devil's Claws

Odiel's mother had forbidden him to speak to his grandfather. He didn't know much about the old man except that he lived in a mansion with servants. He imagined that they served him turtle soup, lamprey pies, and bread puddings with nutmeg. What else did he know? Well, he knew that his grandfather drove through the park every day in his carriage with a set of wheels that were said to be made out of gold. Odiel often hid himself behind the bushes in the hopes of catching a glimpse of the mysterious man whose blood ran through his veins.

On beautiful summer days, his grandfather would leave his carriage at home and walk his giant mastiff while sporting a chic overcoat, tie, and top hat. Though the sun was shining brightly today, Odiel's grandfather did not come. He didn't know why he thought he would. He was in the kitchen yesterday when his aunt told his mother that the old man had died. He wanted to cry, but his mother forbade him from shedding a single tear. He wasn't worth it, she had said.

As Odiel walked to the mansion, he wondered in which room his grandfather was waiting to be transported to the church and eventually to his grave. He probably lay on a four-poster bed in a room with floors covered by silk rugs. What a sad sight it must be! With crystal chandeliers that were no longer required since his grandfather was now forever in the darkness and an ornate fireplace that no longer needed to warm his old body since he would now be forever cold.

Odiel noticed that ravens were flying in and out of a window

that was slightly ajar. He wished
he was a raven, too, so he could
fly inside and offer his grandfather
his last respects. He knew his
mother would not allow him to
attend the funeral. She had even
rejected her inheritance, claiming
that everything belonged to the
devil. One had to be truly
deranged to say no to such a
fortune.

   "You're one of his family members, aren't you?" Odiel looked
up at the man who approached him. He wore a livery and lit a
cigarette.

   "What's it to you?"

   "I was his footman. You must be pleased he's gone. We all
are."

   "Pleased? How dare you be so insolent? Would you be
pleased if your grandfather died?" Odiel was glad he couldn't
lift the marble lions that stood in front of his grandfather's
mansion, or he would have thrown them at the man.

   "Oh, no, but then my grandfather is too busy to make pacts
with the devil. He hides in his shed most of the time with some
nails and a hammer."

   "How dare you accuse my grandfather of making a pact with
the devil!"

   "You think those ravens are ravens? They're not! They're
little flying fiends who work for the devil, and they're the only
ones who mourn your grandfather's passing."

   "You should be scared of the words that are flying out of your
mouth."

   "You've never met him, have you? Your grandfather told
everyone who would listen that his death was approaching. He
told everyone not to worry if his corpse disappeared as he

belonged to the devil. And he left instructions for what to do when his evil corpse cannot be found. He told us to fill his coffin with stones so that his tainted name wouldn't ever affect his family members who are living a virtuous life. But I'm guessing he didn't mean you."

"It's not your place to guess."

"He will live on in the claws of the devil," the man said, tossing his cigarette on the ground, "that's what that grandfather of yours said."

Odiel saw more ravens approaching from the far distance. They all flew to the mansion. He wondered why everyone thought making a deal with the devil was so bad. His grandfather had wealth and influence, and he doubted he had ever worked a day in his life. Odiel wasn't looking forward to becoming a carpenter as his mother wished him to do. He had heard that the best way to meet the devil was to go to a crossroads at midnight. And why shouldn't he at least listen to what the devil has to say? After all, what's the worst that can happen?

ENDNOTES

We've already seen that lots of witches haunt Flanders, and this is also true for devils. As Flemish folklorist K.C. Peeters wrote, "not without reason does the Dutch vernacular know more than two hundred and fifty different names for the idea of the devil."* Of all the folktales in which the devil plays the main role, "The Blue Barn" is quite a common one, of which many variants exist. Usually, a farmer doesn't have enough room to store his grain and either wittingly or unwittingly makes a pact with the devil. The devil promises to build a barn in one night, and all he wants in exchange is the farmer's soul. In most of these tales, the farmer needs to be rescued by his wife, who claps loudly in her hands and wakes up the rooster. "The Ship's Log" is inspired by the story of a captain blessed with an ever-present stroke of good luck. But a sinister secret is responsible for his good luck. He had forged a pact with the devil. His good luck ran out when, one night, the devil rode in his carriage over the waves to his ships and murdered him in cold blood. The source doesn't mention the devil's motives, but it can be assumed that the captain's time was up and that his soul belonged to the devil. "The Count Who Married the Devil" is told through the point of view of a spirit as a narrative device and doesn't appear in the original folktale. The story shows the full extent of havoc the devil can wreak. If there's one thing the devil shouldn't be able to do, it is enter churches, but our devil in "Battle for a Soul" succeeds in doing the impossible. According to the original source, many people witnessed this fierce battle. "The Gatekeeper of Hell" is also a tale of which many variants exist. In many folktales in which the devil pays wages or offers someone money, the gold they have received turns out to be worthless. The moral of these kinds of stories can only be that it is a waste of time to sign a contract with the prince of darkness. Our last tale in this chapter, "The Devil's Claws," is inspired by a folktale in which a family believes that their deceased relative is being haunted by fiends who have shapeshifted into ravens. This man was said to live a sinful life, and it was thought he had made a pact with the devil. Before the family can bury him, his body disappears, and they have no other option but to fill the coffin with stones. It's also whispered that he never truly died, for he lived on in the claws of the devil himself. As we have seen in this chapter, carriages are very much loved by the devil. You may also have noticed the number of times crossroads are mentioned. They're the place to be if you wish to make a deal with him. The devil appears there at midnight, and in many folktales, people take chickens with them to the crossroads in the hope that the devil is then aware that he has a visitor who wishes to speak with him.

*Peeters, K.C. (1946) *Eigen Aard*, Antwerpen, Drukkerij-uitgeverij De Vlijt.

Lost Souls of
Water and Air

The Church in the Lake

Marthe strolled across the fields. There had been a fair last week, and she knew that people who had walked between the long grass and dandelions had lost their little treasures. She knew because she had enchanted the field by sprinkling a concoction of crushed acorns, motherwort, and the blood of a rooster over the grass. It was something she often did. She had sewn many shawls out of lost handkerchiefs, ribbons, and bonnets, wound many threads into lace with her bobbins, and even melted iron objects and reshaped them into bowls.

Today, Marthe didn't want linen or cotton. She wanted something to eat. Beans perhaps or a nice crust of bread, although she doubted that many people had brought their own food with them to the fair. They sold sausages and cream puffs there, so why would they? She hoped for their sake that they had had the sense to take something edible with them.

Ever since the villagers had discovered that Marthe was a witch, the bakery no longer wanted to sell her bread, and the butcher had said he would rather nail his own son to a cross than let her have a succulent piece of meat.

She was hungry, but she wasn't starving. She grew peas and cabbages in her garden, but if she had to eat greens one more time, she would scream so loudly that the sound of her own shriek would send her to an early grave. Marthe spied something glittering between the blades of grass. A ring.

"Useless," she said before slipping it into her pocket. Next, she found a leather satchel and a pair of scissors a bit farther away, both of which she felt were equally useless. On the other side of the field, she found a cord. It was not something that could be cooked either, but the way it was woven was unlike anything she had ever seen before. It didn't just have three twisted strands as cords usually have, but it had eleven strands of figures woven into it. She recognized the figures of a lamb and a dove and other creatures with snouts and paws that she wanted to study later. She put the cord in her pocket along with an old cup that lay next to it and started to make her way back.

Still, she had nothing to eat besides peas and cabbages. She remembered that there was a spell in one of her books somewhere on how to open doors and enter houses. She was going to try it that evening and hoped to empty her neighbor's kitchen cupboards. They had six children and were bound to have something tasty in their kitchen, perhaps even some leftover cream puffs from the fair.

The pocket in her skirt felt heavier than she thought it should be, and she cupped her hand under it because she was afraid the weight might tear the fabric. If she had brought a needle with her, it wouldn't have been an issue, as she would have been able to sew the cloth back together in only two minutes. She really hoped the fabric would hold as a little voice in her head told her that if the villagers saw her returning with all her little, stolen treasures visible for everyone to see, they would demand that the authorities start to burn witches again, especially if they recognized their own lost items clutched in her arms.

Marthe stopped. She was out of breath. Her pocket had grown so heavy now that it felt as if she was pulling a carriage with the devil inside out of the ground. She glanced behind her. She was pulling something out of the ground, but it wasn't the devil's carriage. If only it had been. She was pulling an entire church out of the ground that was attached to the eleven-strand cord in her pocket.

"You shan't take me," Marthe shouted as she let go of the cord, "oh…my poor eyes…my head…I cannot abide the sight of crosses, and in the devil's name, I command you to sink back

into the ground." she shouted at the church, then fell back down. She averted her eyes and took a deep breath before she stared at where the church had been in the same way as someone who had just seen the ugliest of monsters.

The church was gone. She stood back up, barely having time to process what had just happened before a terrible thunderstorm broke loose. Hundreds of lightning bolts struck the field within seconds. Bewildered, Marthe looked around her, then ran across the field as the sky grew so dark it might as well have been night. It was a darkness she usually loved, but not under these circumstances. In the darkness, there were supposed to be cats, owls, and hares dancing around trees, not lightning strikes that wanted to kill witches. The ground shuddered violently, sending Marthe sprawling into the mud. She clutched the grass with both her hands and cursed God for having made the grass susceptible to tearing. The devil would have had the wits to make it unbreakable. The ground continued to shudder, and she realized she was sinking into a deep hole. As she sank deeper beneath the earth, the only thing she could see was the roots of trees and the worms and millipedes that lived in them. The sky was no longer there. Marthe was alone in a darkness that was too terrifying even for witches.

***

Marthe wanted to die, but to her horror, she continued to live and breathe in the dark hole. As the years went by, it eventually dawned upon her that she would never have her greatest desire. Death would never come. She would live forever in this gloomy labyrinth of roots and rocks. She slept in a dark corner where she had made herself a hard bed from the earth and was careful never to look to the right. There, the church still lay. Her act of pulling the cord out of the ground had not only doomed her, but it had also created a lake above the ground. The quiet days when she slept and bemoaned her fate were nothing compared to the days when it stormed. The sound of lightning woke up the church, and hundreds of voices sang palms as Marthe screamed. She knew the people who were fortunate enough to see the sky could hear her screams and the voices…oh…those horrible voices, but not even the devil had the power to save her now.

KLUDDE AND THE FERRYMAN

"Oh, ferryman! Ferryman! I need to cross," a husky voice shouted from the other side of the river. The ferryman put his sandwiches back in his bag. Three times, he had attempted to eat them, but every time he was about to take a bite, someone needed to cross the river. He took up the oars and rowed the wooden ferry boat to the other side of the river. It had grown dark, but he preferred to work in the darkness. The water streaming down the river sounded like a soothing lullaby to his ears, and the cold breeze that brushed his cheeks was more than welcome after a hot summer's day. He docked and tethered the boat to a pole near the riverbank.

"Do you have any luggage?" he asked the shadow who was standing beneath the trees, some distance away from the boat.

"Baha! Sure, you can take my luggage," the figure walked forward and tossed two heavy sacks of flour into the boat, "but I can cross the river myself!"

"Oh, not you again! I swear I'll kill you one day!" the ferryman clenched his fists and stamped his foot on the ground, "I'll attach heavy blocks of concrete to your limbs and throw you into the river."

Kludde had been pestering the ferryman for over a year. He shouted that he needed to cross one day in a hoarse voice and the next day in a brittle one so that the ferryman would never know if there was a real passenger waiting or not.

"You would risk being decapitated for me? That's a wonderful compliment, dear ferryman, but I can't be killed."

"They wouldn't punish me! They would give me a medal!"

"Baha! If you want to be decapitated, all you have to do is ask.

It would be my pleasure to assist you." Kludde dived into the water with a deafening screech.

The ferryman climbed into his boat and unwrapped his sandwiches once again for what he hoped would be the last time.

"He's at it again, isn't he?" a fisherman approached the boat.
"There's no stopping that vile creature," the ferryman said.
"Tell me about it. He's been starving me and my family."
"Starving? How so?"

"When I drop my nets into the water, he claws at them until they're ridden with holes, and all the fish swim out. He doesn't even have to do that. I often see him in the shape of a dog or a cat, and every time I look into his horrible eyes, I know I won't catch anything that day."

"You're in luck," the ferryman said, "Kludde has just dropped two bags of flour in my boat. Take them home with you."

"Well, I'll be damned, thank you very much, mate." he grabbed both bags and disappeared into the dark woods.

The ferryman finally took a bite of one of his sandwiches. The brown bread stuffed with lots of ham and butter melted in his mouth, but just when he was about to take a second bite, he heard a hoarse voice shout from the other side of the river.

"Oh, ferryman! Ferryman! I need to cross!"

THE WHITE LADY

They say my eyes are too pretty. I'm pure evil. They also say I'm a murderess and use the blood, hair, and bones of those I have killed to brew potions that transform those I dislike into ants and flies. I have no such power, but I won't deny that an unearthliness that many dread surrounds me. It's a blessing. It means I can live alone in the woods with my spiders. But those who fear me are right about one thing: my eyes are too pretty.

I was born in 1789 in Bruges. My mother did not survive giving birth to me, and my father had more important things on his mind than taking care of a daughter. I wound up at the *spellewerkschool* where I learned to make bobbin lace. I turned fine linen threads into garlands of roses, leaves, and trefoils. Some call it magic, the way in which the bobbins roll, the needles prick the cushion, and the pattern grows. Years, I spent practicing, often cursing the night for robbing me of my eyesight.

I left the school in 1806. I bid the schoolmistresses and nuns who had been my companions for years farewell and entered a world where a woman on her own was viewed with suspicion. I was dangerous. My bobbins and pins helped me to survive. I didn't earn much, but I didn't need much, and I was content living a quiet life and not knowing anything about the people who lived next to me.

I was murdered in the winter of 1808. They found my body in a narrow alley. My throat was slit, and my lips were frozen by the snow that had fallen during the night. I was dead, but I still walked. I walked behind my body wrapped in a shroud, and there were many things I saw that I wished I could unsee. I watched the gravediggers toss my body into an unmarked grave. I drifted back to the street where I had lived, past the smiles and sparkling eyes of the crowd. There was a murderer in their midst, but they were relieved that the woman who had dared to be different was no longer there. I heard them say that my eyes were too pretty, that there was a hint of waywardness in them, wickedness. They read evil and impious behavior in my dark green irises. Dead or alive, I no longer wanted to be there. I turned my back and walked away from the city, far away, and went to the woods, and there in the woods I remained.

While in the forest, I remembered a story that was often told in the *spellewerkschool* about the origin of lace. It was said an impoverished girl was strolling in the woods and became enthralled when she saw a spider weaving its web. She went home and succeeded in imitating the spider's fine threadwork. Soon, wealthy ladies from all over Flanders knocked on her door and asked her to create the wonders she had seen in the forest.

I searched for the spiders and found them in a dark cave. The spiders and I slept when the sun shone, and when night fell, we left the hard, damp rocks, danced around the beeches and maples, and made lace together. It was a land of wonder where webs showed the most intricate patterns. The raindrops that clung to them reminded me of pearls, much more valuable than the real ones that often graced the necks of wealthy women in the city.

But sometimes we were disturbed. Sometimes, men would wander in the woods. They were often drunk or miserable or both. When they came too close to the wonders we had created, I would fly after them in a white lace dress adorned with ruffles. They would look into my pretty eyes, become enchanted, and walk with me. We would go deeper and deeper into the woods, but as soon as I saw the first signs of daylight appear, I would

fly back to my cave, and the men despaired. They were now lost in the forest. Alone.

One night, the spiders and I had a visitor, and I did what I always did. This time, there was something not right in this man's heart. Violence dwelt within him. There was something horrendous in his countenance, even though he looked just like any other man, and when he held my hand, a feeling of unspeakable horror overtook me. His hands…his fingers…his thumb, there was an oval-shaped birthmark on his thumb. I had seen his hand before. This was the same hand that had slit my throat.

I walked with him to the pond.

"Do you know what lives here?" I asked.

"Mosquitos, fish, frogs, and so on. The animals you usually find in a pond."

"A water devil," I said, "who devours those who come near the water. It's said his victims suffer for days as he sucks out their blood and eats every bit of flesh hanging on their bones."

"That's a bit macabre," he said, "I have a bottle of brandy at home. Come with me. What do you think?"

"I know who you are, murderer," I said as I pushed him into the pond. I watched joyfully as the hands of the devil grabbed his collar and I closed my eyes to listen to the most beautiful song I had ever heard. His screams, his cries, his shrieks.

I danced around the dead trees and flew over the water for three nights. I laughed every time I saw the devil throwing a bone into the grass, but then the music stopped, and a tear rolled down my cheek. He no longer suffered.

The night I pushed him into the pond, I became more than a ghost. I transformed into the sorceress who fed the devil. Soon, the story was whispered into human ears far and wide, and nobody dared to go into the forest anymore. Now, my spiders and I endlessly weave the lace that adorns the trees without ever being disturbed, and the spiders whisper to those who stare at

the trees: don't go into the woods, don't go into the woods. The
sorceress's eyes are pretty, but dead.

The Woman in the Wind

I sat down on a tree stump and sighed. Lost. Me? Lost in the woods? Beyond the realm of possibility! That's what it is. Pffff…lost? I had often played hide and seek in these woods as a child. I used to pretend to be Ambiorix defeating the Romans while running from tree to tree, and once I had even been Caesar himself as I stood on a rock and loudly proclaimed that the Belgae are the bravest of all the Gauls. How could I be lost?

The onset of the night was near, and since there were so many dark clouds in the air, I knew the moon would bring little comfort. Its silvery beams of light would never touch the leaf-strewn earth. I cursed myself for having visited my parents so late in the day and then choosing to take the scenic route through the forest instead of treading the familiar dusty gravel road.

I contemplated what would bring me the greatest hardship on this cold autumn night. Sleeping against a tree to wake up in horror the following morning to find that I had been sleeping on an ant's nest with beetles and centipedes crawling over my legs? Or wandering the pitch-black forest and waking up creatures that even my worst nightmares don't dare to disturb? I buried my head in my knees. The impending night turned the orange, yellow, and red leaves beneath my boots to gray, and soon they would become as black as mud. But something was not right. The leaves were moving, twirling around in circles. Not because of crawling insects but because of something far more sinister.

I jumped up from the tree stump and fled to the shelter of an oak tree. There, I watched in horror. The leaves seemed to have souls. The wind lived inside them as they swirled to form a round tower until, slowly, the wind became a woman. She flew in my direction, and I ran. I ran as swiftly as possible, but have you ever tried to run in a dark forest? Everything, from fallen trees and sharp stones to thorn bushes, is out for your blood.

The woman followed me. Her icy cold hands pulled at my hair, and her sharp nails dug into my skin as she tried to grab my arms. She flew quicker than I could run, and once she reached me, she threw me to the ground.

***

When I finally woke up, the unsettling darkness of the night had made way for the soothing presence of the sun. My head was bursting, and on my legs, I saw the unearthly burning red handprints where the ghostly wind had snatched at me. I vaguely remembered a song from my youth.

> *I feel that I must go*
> *Flying in the winds*
> *As long as the world exists*
> *And never find any solace**

Oh, Alvina, were you the wind yesterday? I know the stories. It's said that Alvina was cursed to live forever in the wind. My parents often said that when the wind howls, Alvina is weeping. Or was it any of the other women who have been cursed to the same fate? There are tales of a woman who makes dust fly into the air and blinds the eyes of the unlucky people who encounter her. She is also the wind who throws grain and flax into the air during the summer months and ruins harvests. Then, there is yet another woman in the wind who forms whirlwinds around hapless souls and carries them away. She's the worst of all, for it's said that when she appears, the devil is dragging someone to hell. Thank God, I'm still here, but if it was she, whose soul is now perishing in the fires of hell?

*Part of an old Flemish folk song translated from J.R.W. Sinninghe's collection of Flemish folktales. (Sinninghe, J.R.W. (1948) Oude Volksvertellingen, Oisterwijk, Uitgeverij Oisterwijk).

The Carriage of Hell

"It's nearly midnight. We must hide," Pieter said.

"How do you even know it exists?" Charlotte asked, but she wrapped their one-year-old son in a blanket anyway and descended into the cellar."

"I've seen it with my own eyes, Charlotte. It nearly took me once."

"So you keep telling me, but since we're sheltering in the cellar every night, I would like to know what exactly happened."

"Only if you promise to never ask me about it again," Pieter said while he bolted the cellar door.

"I promise."

"I was ten, and I was afraid of falling asleep. Nightmares had been terrorizing me for seven days in a row, and in them, frightful demons clad in white appeared. Their misty hands grabbed my legs and arms as they pulled me into the skies and tore my flesh from my bones. Not wanting to enter that world again, not even in sleep, I went outside and sat on the pavement. I stared at the bright moon and the stars. There was a strong wind, but besides that, it was a quiet night. All of a sudden, I heard children chanting. It was a strange melody that seemed to belong to another world. Their voices were so high, so dreamy, and so utterly beautiful. Then, I saw a carriage pulled by four horses who blew fire out of their nostrils. A carriage of which the clopping sound of horses' hooves could not be heard while they struck the cobbled streets because they didn't touch the ground. The carriage flew. I thought it was magic, and it is magic, but it is the darkest, most unholy magic in existence. The carriage stopped before me and I looked at the children who were chanting inside the coach box. They wore long white dresses like the ones you see choir children wear in church. Their skin was pale, and then I saw that worms and beetles crawled in the empty sockets of their eyes while a swarm of flies circled around them. They started to climb out of the carriage. They wanted me. But before they could drag me inside that hellish wagon, my grandfather appeared and pulled me back inside the house."

"Why does it take children?"

"My grandfather told me that the carriage is the art of the devil. It was born in the fires of hell. It takes children and murders them. It forces them to sing while the carriage flies through the streets of Bruges. And I'll be damned if my son becomes one of them."

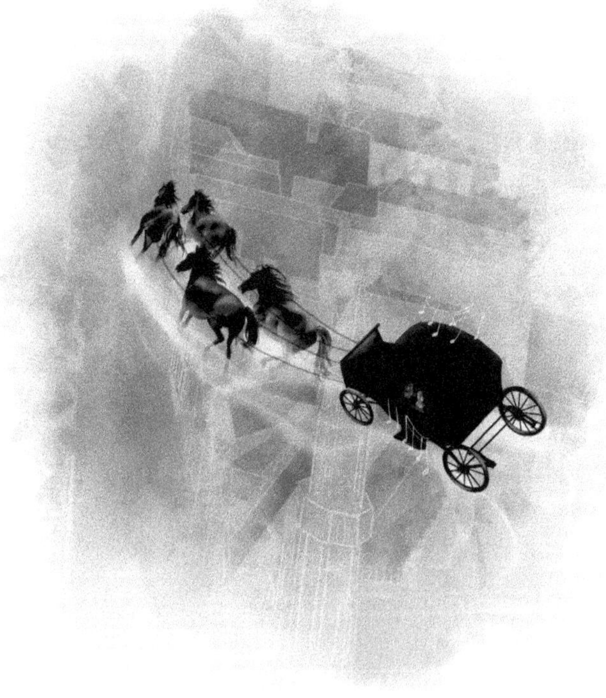

Damned Souls

She placed the ladder against the wall and climbed on the roof. Just like the storm, she was furious. Furious that she was the one who had to shovel the snow off the roof as the cold wind clawed her rosy cheeks and the icy temperatures turned her fingers blue. Yesterday, the freezing rain that had tormented the countryside for weeks had changed into hail, then into sleet, and then into what she abhorred most of all: snow. The garden fence, the leafless maple trees, and the cobblestone road were covered in a layer of sparkling snow. She had heard many call it beautiful. If only they looked up and saw what they pretended not to see. The ominous and baleful gray sky. It made her feel uneasy, and even the robins who usually sang in the hedges did not make a sound. Not one. Not even a melancholy chirp.

She pushed the shovel into the soft snow. Soft but so heavy that her shovel quivered as she dropped a first load into the garden below. The wind seemed to form an invisible circle around her and screeched. No, it didn't just screech. It howled and screamed. It felt as if the wind was running away. She fantasized it was spring. The wind would continue to run, and so would the nightmarish being that pursued it. The wind would hide in a barn only to discover that the shadowy figure it had been running from was holding an axe and staring into the wind's heart. It would be the last thing it saw. Wind and winter would return no more, and next year, she would be walking in daisy fields instead of shoveling snow.

She laid the shovel down and listened to the sounds surrounding her. That wind. It cried out as an unearthly chorus of voices. She thought she could hear wailing and harrowing laments. Voices. Voices promising they will never steal again if only someone would rescue them, they will never commit arson again if only someone would take pity and end their suffering, they will never commit murder again if only someone would release them. They beg. For forgiveness, redemption, and salvation. Sometimes, when they think there might be hope, their voices are gentle, almost sweet, but then they howl once more. Warmth and sympathy will never embrace them.

She picked up the shovel again and thought of her grandmother. Before she passed away, she had said that the souls of the dead live in the wind. They wake you in the middle of frigid winter nights, their tortured screams echoing through your home. They follow you when you venture outside.

Sometimes, when it's snowing, when the air feels rageful as a storm ravages the countryside, like today, the words that the cursed voices speak can be deciphered. The doomed hopes and fears of damned souls enter the unwilling ears of those who are still breathing, and as she shoveled, she prayed that her grandmother wasn't one of them.

ENDNOTES

Many folkloric beings live in water and air. They are mysterious, and those who lurk in rivers and creeks are known to drag wanderers or those who make the mishap of dragging a church out of the ground to a watery grave. The piercing cries of those who dwell in the wind slice through one's bone to the marrow. They are beings we would not like to meet, but at the same time, a veil of dark enchantment surrounds them, captivating us and making us wish we could unravel their secrets. The witch in "The Church of the Lake" doubtlessly wishes that she hadn't unraveled those secrets. There are many Flemish folktales about churches and monasteries that have sunk into the ground. In one such tale, God himself sinks a monastery into the ground because the monks lived what he deemed to be a sinful life. They must not have cared very much since they can still be heard feasting from the darkness in which they have been thrust. It's also said that the clocks of drowned churches can often be heard, especially on Christmas Eve. "The Church in the Lake" is a unique one since a witch actually pulls a church out of the ground and then suffers a horrendous fate. It can be safely assumed that her action of creating a lake was of little comfort to her. Kludde is a shapeshifter who appears in many guises and often torments those who have the misfortune of meeting him. He's such an important figure in Flemish storytelling traditions that he will appear once more in this book, but here, he's a pesky water creature who seeks amusement through a harmless, albeit annoying prank. "The White Lady" is inspired by a tale of a woman who was said to ensure that men got either lost in the woods or who delivered them to the waterdevil who lived in a pond. The story also mentions a legend from Bruges that says that a girl invented the craft of lacemaking after she saw spiders weaving their webs in the woods. Belgium's acclaim for its lace industry also means that much folklore surrounds this art form, and some even thought that those skilled workers were witches. It's noteworthy to mention that Venice also has a legend in which it is claimed lace originated in Italy's more famous City of Canals.

The wind often sings haunting songs, and it is, therefore, natural that folktales regarding unearthly beings who live in the wind developed. "The Woman in the Wind" is inspired by a story in which a man is kicked to the ground by a woman who lives in the wind and then goes on to mention several other figures who were said to dwell in the wind. In the "Carriage of Hell," we have a ghostly carriage from which it is best to stay far away, and it isn't the only carriage in Flanders that flies around with malevolent and sinister motives. The last tale of this chapter is based on the belief that the voices of damned souls can be heard in the wind on cold winter days.

Ghosts

THE HOUSE IN THE SEA

The man who needed good luck had once been happy. He remembered the blissful days when he had walked to the harbor in the morning hours. He greeted everyone he met along the way with a smile, whether they were two ladies chatting on a bench or dozens of gulls greedily swallowing earthworms. He wasn't a wealthy man, but he always caught just enough mackerel, whiting, and cod to feed his wife and children, and that was all he wanted. He had once heard someone say that things change, and they were right. Things did change. He was no longer a happy man.

The bad luck that began to haunt him first appeared on a rainy afternoon. The fish refused to be lured into his nets. At that time, he was still the kind of person who didn't easily give in to despair, and he returned the following day with an even bigger smile on his face. But a month later, when he had still not caught a single fish, he let out a cry of anguish.

Cries of anguish would soon be the only sound that left his lips. His wife and children died when the waves cruelly dragged them into the deep after he had taken them on a trip on his boat. It had been a sunny and windless morning, but the sea suddenly decided that it wanted blood. Consumed by grief, the man wandered the streets aimlessly.

He no longer smiled and eventually became convinced that he was being followed. Not by the legions of shapeshifters that were known to fill the region with terror but by a single shadow that wished him ill, a shadow that wanted him to suffer and shed tears, that wanted him to fail and to obliterate every last shred of hope that still lived in his mind.

The man often wandered to the dunes, and while he was there, he begged God to put him out of his misery. But even there, he found no hope, for as he stared at the tempestuous sea, his heart continued to beat. It confirmed his conviction that God was absent for the inconsolable and dejected, the cheerless and dispirited, and especially for those who needed their creator the most.

One evening, he saw blue sparkling flames dancing over the sea in the far distance. He closed his eyes, thinking he was hallucinating. But when he opened his eyes, he was surprised to see that the flames were still there. It reminded him of a story told by a fellow fisherman a long time ago about a treasure hidden in the seagrass where mysterious lights dance. The fisherman had gone on to say that the only reason nobody had ever claimed this treasure was because nobody knew how to find it.

The man who needed good luck thought about the many other tales he had heard fishermen tell each other. There was one about a ship that had returned to the harbor because a black cat was sleeping in the hold. There was the ghost of a drowned man. The fishermen had found his lifeless body floating in the sea and had taken his body aboard but had been haunted by his spirit when they neglected to return the dead man's pocket watch to his family. Then there were the sailors who carried the bones of hanged thieves with them because they believed the magic that lived in these charms would ensure the voyage would be a good one.

Suddenly, the man felt that someone was watching him. He turned around. A tall, transparent figure with eyes that burned like glowing goals gazed into the man's sunken eyes.

"Don't be afraid," the figure said, "I'm sympathetic to your suffering."

"I don't need sympathy from a ghost," the man said.

"Take this enchanted ring. Wear it and walk through the sea to the spot where the blue flames are dancing. Don't let yourself be distracted by anything you encounter along the way. At the end of the path, you will find a jar. It's yours. Take it, and then run for the shore as quickly as you can."

"Fool someone else and let me be," the man who needed good luck said. His words had the desired effect—the sands rose and swallowed the figure up. The man threw the ring into the sea and went homeward. The next day, he knew that bad luck was still following him. He became ill with a fever and couldn't leave his bed for weeks. When he finally regained some of his strength and ventured to the dunes, he soon wished he had never left his house. He returned to find his house on fire and watched in horror as it burned to the ground. He cursed himself for not having burned with it. Things did indeed change, he thought to himself, just not how he wished them to change.

Without a roof over his head or a penny in his pocket, he was forced to sleep on the dunes. He began to hope that the ghost would appear again. After three nights, the apparition revealed itself and offered him the ring once more.

The man who needed good luck felt that the wind would bring a storm forth soon. He knew very well that the waves have no mercy for people who are caught up in tempests, but it was his only chance to find some good luck again. Failing that, a grave in the sea sounded like an appropriate ending to his story.

He walked along the beach and slipped the ring on his finger before he entered its cruel waters. His heart beat faster when, all of a sudden, the sea opened itself to reveal a cobbled road leading to a land that lay in the middle of the waves.

On the road, he saw the familiar faces of people he had once greeted on the streets. He wanted to shake their hands and strike up a conversation with them just as he used to do until he remembered that they had all drowned a long time ago.

At the end of the road, a grassy plot of land appeared. There, in the middle of the sea, was a red house with stepped gables,

dark blue gutters, and white embroidered curtains. The door opened, and his wife and four children waited for him on the threshold. He wanted to run to them, embrace them, cover them in kisses, and never let them go again. But then he remembered what the ghost had said. *Don't let yourself be distracted.* With tears in his eyes, he turned his back on those he loved most.

He found the jar hidden between rocks and seagrass. The seabed trembled when he picked it up. He thought he would become one of them. A drowned soul. Perhaps the ghost had led him here because there was a life for him in the sea, a life with his family. Perhaps they would be together again? But he knew it was not to be since the ghost had told him to return, and now there was anger in the eyes of his children as they watched him.

The man walked back toward the shore. The drowned souls followed him. They wept, pleading with him to remain. When he ignored them, they began to screech. Their cold, watery hands brushed his neck, his torso, and his legs as angry voices howled from the darkness. With every step he took, their cries grew more menacing. But as the ghost advised, the man tried not to let himself be distracted. He wasn't sure he was going to make it, so he quickened his pace until he ran faster than he had ever done in his entire life.

Once his feet touched the sand on the beach, the sea closed, leaving his wife and four children behind him forever.

He opened the jar. It contained gems and gold, but the most valuable thing could be found at the bottom: good luck. The man bought a lavish townhouse. He spent his days reading and writing down the little adventures that transpired while he was still a fisherman and the stories he had heard people tell. He was alive, and being alive was bearable, but he could still not call himself a happy man. Not without his loved ones. The man who needed good luck never forgot his ghostly benefactor and often returned to the dunes in the hopes of meeting him again and asking him if there was any way for his family to join him, but neither the ghost nor the blue flames ever reappeared.

An earlier version of this folktale was published on the website
of SuperstitionSam (https://superstitionsam.com) as A Flemish
Fairy Tale Retelling: The Man Who Needed Good Luck.

The Eternal Fisher

"I know you mean well, but they're liars, ma," I said as I led my horse out of the stables and tucked the fishing nets into my bag, "the church needs fear to survive, and that's what they're feeding you. Fear. And you're eating out of their hands, but I'm warning you, it's poison."

"There's a reason why it's forbidden to fish on Easter. People have disappeared."

"It's a load of rubbish. They don't want any empty chairs at church. That's their reason."

"You don't believe the priests? Believe the witches. Even they remain in their cottages because they know very well they would get themselves cursed if they went to the sea today."

"If someone is going to curse me, I'll happily drag my net through the sea until the end of times," I said, "but I promise you'll see me for dinner this evening."

"Please, you're my only child. Don't go. Do it for me."

"I'm doing this for you, ma," I said as I mounted my horse, "what else are you going to eat? Sand?"

The beach was empty, and rain-filled clouds were gathering in the distance, but the sea was still. There were no waves, only small ripples played across the water's surface. Once my horse's hooves touched the foamy water, she stopped and refused to move forward. I dismounted.

"Come on, you old girl," I tried to push her into the sea, but she snorted and tried to back up. Oh dear, my horse had become my mother. Superstitious. The silly beast now believed that singing in the morning would result in tears in the evening or that a salt cellar falling over meant that a violent argument would follow. My mother even avoided going outside in the early hours of the morning because she feared that if sailors saw a woman before going on their journey, they would be wrecked at sea, and it would all be her fault. But the horse wasn't my mother. She couldn't be. And today was a good day to fish for shrimp on horseback. She must go into the sea.

I gave her a pat on her rear end, and at last, she began to move forward. She waded knee-deep into the water when, all of a sudden, a storm broke loose. It seemed as if God himself had sent the lightning, and the sea that had been so still became a raging monster. My horse and I were pushed beneath the waves, and everything went black as I lost consciousness.

When I awoke, I was seated on my horse, but there was something wrong, something different. Neither my horse nor I had a heartbeat. I was shivering. My hands looked pale. The seawater had wrinkled them beyond recognition. When I looked at the beach, I realized my horse and I were standing in the sea. It was night. I tried to recall what my mother looked like, but all I could remember was a distant shadow from another world. I now understood that my horse and I belonged to the water, that we were cursed to use the terrible temperament of the sea to strike terror into the hearts of those who were yet breathing.

We are now horrifying entities. But lest someone judge us, isn't that what ghosts are supposed to be? From that day forward, my horse and I walk through the sea in search of innocent victims. When I gaze deeply into their eyes, they soon become enchanted. They lose their free will and have no other choice but to follow me deeper and deeper into the sea until they drown. I am the eternal fisher. Doomed to fish for souls instead of shrimp, and once I have them in my thrall, I drown them in the salty water. Yes, corpses swirl and float around me. The gulls pick them apart, and eventually, their bones sink to the seabed. But I am still here. I walk with my horse through the sea.

BOKKENRIJDERS

Am I a ghost? Am I a demon? Am I a madman with a goat? I don't fairly know myself. I don't remember when I was born, and neither can I recall if I have died. The only thing I do know is that the woman I love is buried in a grave that is two hundred years old.

I remember attending her funeral. She was so young. We were going to marry. She wanted two children, a rose garden, and a house with two chimneys, but cholera killed her dreams.

I started to think about God and how he was never at my side, how he bullied me by pouring buckets of misery and hardship over my head, and I cursed him for killing my future.

Then I said the most ungodly words imaginable. *I renounce God and worship the devil. I renounce God and worship the devil. I renounce God and worship the devil.* Three times. I'm not certain why I decided to worship the devil. I think I just wanted to hurt the monster who dwells in heaven in the most painful way. I'm quite sure he didn't listen; he never does, but it didn't matter. The devil listened.

The devil gave me a goat. Not just any goat…oh no…a flying goat! I called him *Hellevorst*, after the dapper prince who dwells in the fires of hell. All I have to do is climb on the goat's back, say 'over hedges and bushes,' and the goat flies high into the air through violent storms and windless skies alike. Those brave enough to witness my flight can be seen waving on the ground below, but those whom I really love are the terrified ones. They are the cowards who hide in their homes during the magical hour when the sky belongs to goats and their riders. And while they tremble, I chortle and snigger.

One night, after I had drained too many bottles of a fine red wine that I had stolen from the cellars of a monastery, I invited a gang of robbers to fly on my goat with me. There were six of us riding on the back of the animal and one on its tail. I have to admit it was uncomfortable at times, and one of the robbers nearly fell off the goat and into the swamp below, but my companions didn't mind. Their days were numbered, the authorities were on to them, and they all agreed that drowning in a swamp after one last night of spectacular fun makes a much better ballad than simply being hung from a noose.

The robbers and I flew over a manor of some lord and saw that his laundry was hanging outside to dry. There were several fancy black waistcoats and white linen shirts. We swooped into the garden and flew away with the lord's clothes. Afterward, I dropped the robbers off in the woods and then flew to Wellen.

If only I had stayed in the forest with them. In Wellen they saw something unnatural in my eyes, and guess where I am now? A damp prison cell. They say they'll burn me for my crimes. Ha! Burn me! Burn a ghost? A demon? Have they thought this through? Can you kill a ghost? And if I am a demon, shouldn't they be afraid the flames will have no effect on me? They may burn me as often as they like. If I do die, I'll be eternally happy, for I'll finally be with the woman I love again. If I don't die, I'll probably just rob another wine cellar.

THE BARON OF VINDERHOUTEN

The baroness looked at the uneven cobblestone walls and the ancient timber door through which so many souls must have entered the castle in days of old. Their hearts had long since stopped beating, but she imagined she could see their shadows flying around the towers and hooded turrets while crows and jackdaws graced the air.

Her eyes strayed to the arrowslits that had once been used by archers to slay besiegers. One of her ancestors had filled them with stones because he had been convinced evil spirits crawled through them. The baroness had read in his journal that he was terrified of being murdered in his sleep, and he was right to be terrified, but the murderer did not come while he was sleeping. The murderer slit his throat while he sat in his fauteuil in front of the fireplace. He had been telling his grandchildren about Reynard the Fox and his archenemy, Ysengrim.

There was no reason to be afraid now. She had inherited the castle and the surrounding lands from a distant uncle with whom she had never even shared a cup of tea. She doubted evil spirits were interested in a baroness struggling to maintain the grounds. She was going to ask the groundskeeper to remove the stones tomorrow.

Tonight, she wanted to see if the fence had been repaired. The wooden walkway that made the marshes accessible groaned as her heels clicked on the boards. Some of the planks were shrunken and discolored, *something else I must tell the groundskeeper*, she thought as she listened to the crickets, frogs,

and mosquitoes sing while they disregarded each other's tunes.

The chaotic dance of cordgrass while the wind fiercely rustled through the blades caught her attention as she followed the elevated path deeper and deeper into the marsh. She stopped when she saw a glowing light floating above the water.

"Come to me, come to me," the light whispered in a piping voice while it playfully darted against the background of a darkening sky. It hid itself behind the reeds only to reappear and glow brighter than it had before.

The baroness did not dare to move because the light seemed to have put her under some sort of spell.

"Be still!" she shouted.

"Are you one of those?" the light asked as it fluttered around her, "one of those people that murder joy?"

"I've heard stories about your kind," she said, "are they true? Are you the soul of an unbaptized child?"

"Why would you like to know?"

"Because I won't be one of your victims," she said, "You're a will-o'-the-wisp, and those who baptize will-o'-the-wisps are pulled into the water and drown. I've heard the stories."

"I'm a messenger of the death," the light dove into the marsh but quickly resurfaced, "and I don't need to be baptized. I'm here in the name of the Baron of Vinderhouten, who was murdered in the year of our Lord 1610. You've read his journal. You know how grisly his death was, and he knew it too — long before it happened. Before the unspeakable occurred, he ordered his servants to fill the moat with grain. It's the duty of his descendants to say as many requiems as there are grains in the water, a duty that now befalls you."

"What? Who did he think he was that he is now required to be remembered three hundred years after his death? The pope? A saint? Or perhaps the Almighty himself?"

"You're one of those who will neglect your duty, aren't you? I love it when that happens." the light giggled before it disappeared into the water once more.

The baroness commanded the light to return. She screamed and shouted until her cries changed into pleas. The light did not come back. She was alone again, the cordgrass still dancing in the wind. The dark clouds gathering in the distance started to creep closer.

The baroness returned to the castle and made herself a cup of tea before she sat down with Georges Rodenbach's *Bruges-la-Morte* in the same fauteuil where a baron had once died. She had fallen in love with the gilded carvings of leaves in the beechwood and the dark blue damask upholstery the first time she saw it, and no dead baron was going to ruin that for her. But the novel remained unopened. She stared at the longcase clock. Waiting. Waiting until it struck eleven and announced that it was the appropriate time to go to bed.

***

The farmer who lived between the village and the castle knew a sleepless night was coming when he saw black clouds gathering above the marshland. He knew they were not filled with rain. His grandfather had told him that the Vinderhouten family was an odd one. They had an ancestor who expected his heirs to obey and honor him even though he died ages ago. Once, a descendant had ignored the wishes of the dead baron. A murky black carriage had descended out of the clouds and driven to the castle. The rumbling wheels had scared the village children, and their parents had crawled beneath the blankets with them. If the carriage were going to drag their children to a horrid realm far above the clouds where beings with rotten flesh that had been half-eaten away by undead vultures were a common sight, they would rather go together.

The farmer shut the door behind him and walked to the castle. It was happening again. Like the ancestor his grandfather had told him about, the baroness had refused to obey the wishes of the dead baron. The sound of his heavy boots thumped on the walkway and echoed around him. He stopped when he saw a man whose skin was as pale as the moon sitting on the castle threshold.

"Good evening," the farmer said, waiting for the man to move aside so that he could knock on the door. But the man didn't respond.

"Good evening," the farmer repeated. He thought it odd that not even the fierce wind had the power to make the long dark brown hair of the man move.

"You will address me as baron," the man said in a cold voice, "or I'll knock you down."

"Do you take me for a fool?" the farmer asked, "I know what the baroness looks like, and you're not her, alright?"

"You will address me as baron," a misty cloud floated from the man's mouth as he spoke. In an instant, the man was now standing so close to the farmer that he could feel the man's icy breath on his skin.

"Someone has to be knocked down?" The farmer said as he lunged for a shovel that leaned against the castle wall. "Fine, then I'll knock you down."

The farmer hit the stranger on the head with the shovel. It should only have left a bump on the man's head, but the shovel continued straight through his body like a knife slicing through a sponge cake. The man was split in half for a moment, but seconds later, a gray vapor swirled around him, and his body was suddenly whole again.

The farmer realized that the man who wanted to be called Baron was the Baron who died in 1610. He ran home as quickly as he could and did not dare to leave his farmstead for weeks out of fear someone had witnessed the chilling encounter. They would call him a murderer. Yes, you cannot murder a ghost, but how was he to know that the figure was a ghost? He was capable of murder, and that was all that mattered.

It took time, a lot of time, but the farmer finally ventured outside once he had run out of food. He was surprised when there were no odd looks and nobody whispered behind his back. He was even more surprised when he bumped into the baroness, and she gave him a friendly nod.

Since the farmer's encounter with the long-dead baron, no more masses had been read for the baron's soul. No black carriages had descended out of the sky, and no ghostly figures or will-o'-the-wisps had been spotted in the marshes. Seven years later, the baroness invited him to dinner and thanked him for killing the unwelcome specter. But the farmer wasn't sure the harrowing encounters with shadowy spirits belonged to the past. There was a strange rabbit in the woods. The animal often wailed and screamed as it hopped from tree to hedge and from hedge to tree. He had tried to shoot the animal several times, but the rabbit always disappeared before the bullet hit the beast. Yes, a beast, for this rabbit was not of this world. The farmer was so sure the beast was the Count of Vinderhouten that he was prepared to cut off his own arm if he was ever proven to be wrong.

THE SKULL

Ernest wondered what those who lay beneath the gravestones looked like, if the clothes they had been buried in had already begun to rot, and if their eyes had already been eaten by worms, or if all that remained were bones, teeth, and hair. He wondered if they had been sinners like he was. If they had also been in the process of gambling their family's fortune away, partaking in extravagant meals of wild swine and pheasants during the forty days of Lent and refusing to contribute to any almsgiving? Probably not. Their headstones were unembellished. Boring. They suggested that the families that the dead had left behind could ill afford the funerals of their loved ones. Ernest could have a mausoleum with stained glass windows, a mosaic floor, and statues of winged cherubs and angels if he wished, but they could feed his body to the crows for all he cared.

Ernest knew there was no heaven or hell. There was no point in having a priest read some ancient texts over a casket. Lies! It was all lies! His soul would not go to heaven or hell. It would remain here on this wretched earth and decompose like the rest of him.

"If there's any life left in you, you're invited for dinner this evening," Ernest said as he kicked a skull that had escaped from its grave and lay on the gravel path. He left the graveyard and walked to his castle. It was a cold, dank place, but he had managed to turn one of the wings into a comfortable corner, leaving the rest of the castle equally comfortable for the spiders and rats who dwelt in dusty, dark, forgotten rooms of old.

Ernest went to the drawing room. He stared at the pendulum clock. It was one his grandfather had bought and decorated with twirled carvings and wooden horses on the top. He wondered how much the clock would fetch in one of Brussels' antique shops. It was where most of his grandfather's furniture had ended up as Ernest was always in need of funds to finance playing vingt-et-un in the kind of back-alley inns his grandfather would have helped to raze to the ground if anyone had given him a sledgehammer. Ernest giggled as he thought of the wrath and rage that would consume his grandfather if only the old man knew what his favorite grandchild had done to his fortune. Ernest slumped into a chair and soon fell into a deep sleep. He woke up when the maid announced that dinner was being served.

As he walked into the lonely dining room, he heard someone knocking at the gates, "if it's *Monsieur* Laisné, tell him I'm not here," he shouted, "I'm going to slam his head in if he requires any more money."

Ernest scoffed at the roses that decorated the table. His mother had always insisted upon flowers in the dining room. Ernest thought flowers had a shorter lifespan than fruit flies, and since they died, they were an unnecessary expenditure. He sat down and opened the newspaper as the maid walked in.

"Get rid of these roses, and don't buy any more flowers," he said without looking up.

"*Monsieur*, there's someone here to see you."

"Someone?" Ernest dropped the paper, "What do you mean someone? You didn't ask for this someone's name? What if you have let in a robber? Or worse, *Monsieur* Laisné?" he noticed that the maid's hands were shaking, and her usual rosy complexion had turned quite pale.

"You invited me for dinner," Ernest stared wide-eyed at the being that stood before him. His guest didn't have any flesh or organs. It was a skeleton.

"What kind of trickery is this?" he loudly exclaimed as he watched the maid run out of the room.

"You kicked against my skull in the graveyard, which is terribly bad manners as far as I'm concerned. But you were, at the same time, kind enough to invite me for dinner."

"You can't…you can't…no, there's no way you're real."

"It looks to me as if your eyes are in good working order. Or has something been affecting your vision?"

"Well…no…but…."

"Then I'm real," the skeleton said as he seated himself.

The maid soon returned with roasted chicken and green beans. Ernest didn't touch the food, but the skeleton said he was starving and cheerfully tucked in. The food immediately vanished when it touched the skeleton's horseshoe-shaped bone underneath his chin.

Ernest's guest helped himself to the bottle of wine on the table and Ernest soon found himself opening another bottle as the skeleton declared that the chicken had made him very thirsty. He clapped his skeletal hands when the maid brought in the orange pudding and devoured it all in one bite.

"I might as well start believing in heaven and hell," Ernest said, running his hands through his hair, "I'll stop gambling, I'll give to the poor, I'll even attend Mass."

"Too late," the skeleton said while he wiped his bones on a tissue, "you're about to find out how real hell is because that's where I'm going to drag you to now."

In loving memory of Lord Ernest
1834-1858
You were taken from us far too soon, never
to be seen again, to the fires of hell.

A Sea of Flames

"You're a good boy," Jean-Pierre stroked the bloodhound's drooping ears, then placed a bowl of chopped sausages in front of him, "but you must stay here when night falls. You never know what might be roaming about, do you? And though you're fierce, your heart is too gentle to consort with the creatures that plague the night."

Bliksem pushed the bowl away with his snout. If dogs could cry actual tears, Jean-Pierre's house would have been drifting on a river by now. The dog had belonged to Jean-Pierre's oldest friend. Evert and he had grown up living only two houses apart and had spent many summers building tree houses and catching tadpoles. As they grew up, the villagers became convinced that Evert was a wizard. Some even said he was immortal. He had been involved in many brawls and scuffles but was never seen with bruised knuckles or a black eye.

Once, he had been squashed by a tree and escaped unharmed by what should have been a horrible death. Then there was that time he lost a bet and drank hemlock tea without suffering the slightest weakness, tremors, or seizures. Some of the villagers were disappointed when they heard Evert had succumbed to a fever, for they all believed that if he weren't immortal, he would die of something weird, something that would be talked about for years to come. Not a boring fever.

Bliksem had not left Evert's bedside while he was ill, and neither had Jean-Pierre. The last story Evert would ever tell was how he had found his beloved bloodhound. It had been a stormy night, and as usual, Evert had been drinking at the inn. When he returned home through the woods, deafening thunder rumbled, and the lightning decided which tree would live and which one would die. Lightning struck an oak tree, and the light allowed him to see a young pup lying curled up underneath a bush. The animal was shaking and trembling. Evert had taken the dog home with him and called him Bliksem after the lightning. Without that storm, they would never have found each other.

Jean-Pierre doubted Bliksem knew that the risk of finding someone was that you could lose them. When Evert was buried three days ago, the dog had whimpered and whined as the coffin in which his owner rested descended into the earth. It was a song of mourning, a song that Bliksem, aside from some brief intervals, hadn't stopped singing.

"I don't want to do this, Bliksem, but I don't have another choice," Jean-Pierre walked to the kitchen and returned with a heavy metal chain. He fastened one end to the dog's leg and attached the other end around the iron grate in front of the fireside. He had thought the bloodhound would protest, but he hadn't even lifted his head.

"Now, you can't go running to the graveyard," Jean-Pierre said, "and I can catch some sleep this evening."

He went upstairs and sank into his bed. He soon found himself in a deep, dreamless sleep, but all of a sudden, something woke him up. It wasn't a noise or someone standing near his bed but a feeling. A feeling that something bad was about to happen. Jean-Pierre went downstairs to check on Bliksem. The chain had broken in two, and the dog was gone. He quickly put on his coat and went outside. It was a moonless night, and though he hadn't carried his kerosene lamp with him, he didn't need light to walk to the graveyard. It was a road that he had trodden more often than he would have liked.

The dog was sitting before Evert's grave. Whining. Weeping. Wailing. Suddenly, a light shone from out of the grave. Something rose to the sky. A white and transparent ghost surrounded by a sea of flames and fire. Bliksem wagged his tail

as the spirit flew higher into the air, and the whole graveyard
was lit by a reddish glow. A hand reached out and stroked the
belly of the bloodhound. Bliksem rolled in the grass and grunted
playfully. When the ghost descended back into the earth,
Bliksem howled.

Jean-Pierre ran to the grave and found the dog fast asleep. No,
not asleep. Bliksem would never wake up again. His master had
risen from the grave to comfort his dog and they were now
together, united forever in death.

ENDNOTES

Of course, a book about folktales can't leave out the ghosts! Ghosts haunt the darkest corners of Flanders, but it should be noted that many of the ghosts encountered in the region are kind. One such tale is "The House in the Sea," where the ghost whom the narrator meets on the beach demonstrates kindness to a miserable man, but in the same tale, we also meet a group of evil phantoms who wish to drown the man. It has already been mentioned that Catholicism is present in many of these tales, and this comes to the foreground in "The Eternal Fisher," who defies the custom of not being allowed to fish on Easter. According to other versions, the ghost of this story wasn't a ghost at all but a witch who had the ability to shapeshift into a crow. Bokkenrijders would have been an excellent fit for the Devil chapter as well, but they ended up with the ghosts. Similar to the many so-called witches who were wrongfully put to death, the bokkenrijders are a tragic subject as men in the 18th century were unjustly accused of riding on goats that flew through the sky, making pacts with the devil and robbing and murdering in his name. Many were sentenced to death. In folktales, they often commit minor crimes like stealing cattle or someone's laundry, and such a tale is included here. "The Count of Vinderhouten" is an odd one. The story jumps from a countess who refuses to say masses for her ancestor to a farmer who 'kills' a ghost and ends with an unearthly rabbit. In "The Skull," it is made clear that even if you do repent your actions, it might be too late, and in "A Sea of Flames", we again meet a kind ghost who wanted to comfort the loyal dog he left behind and who did give the people who lived in the area quite a fright. While most ghost stories are meant to be terrifying, this is often not the case in Flanders. Ghosts often haunt these lands because they have buried a treasure somewhere, and they want a breathing soul to dig that treasure up and give it to either the church or the poor. Only then will they be able to rest in peace.

Unique Beings of Flanders

KLUDDE

Grete ran. She ran through the wheat field. There were no stars in the sky, and the moon was hidden behind a veil of clouds. Mercifully, the light that shone brightly inside the farmhouse guided the way. She ran toward the light, longing to embrace her father, mother, and two little sisters. If the beast killed Grete, her family would be inconsolable. They would be unable to mention her name and wish they could forget she had even existed. The memory of their dead daughter would be unbearable, and their pain would manifest as tears that would soak their pillows each night.

They would never forgive her if they found her bloodied corpse in the wheatfield. She had snuck out of the house and gone to the fair. She had wanted to see the puppet show, the jugglers, the bagpiper who owned a dancing monkey, and most of all, the fortune teller. She told Grete every year that she would be married within twelve months, but she never was.

The beast was still following her. She could hear the creature's paws touching the ground. Thunder. The sound reminded her of thunder. She glanced behind her. A hellish blue light shone out of its eyes. The beast bared its teeth and shook his head, sending drool flying in all directions. Grete felt as if the beast could overtake her if it wanted to, as if it was letting her run merely because it found the sight of terrified humans running for their lives amusing.

If guilt could pull someone into the ground, she would have fallen into a deep hole by now. Her parents had forbidden her to go to the fair because of this beast that crept around at night. They had said that if she wanted to grow old, she should stay near the hearth. Grete had pretended to agree with them, but she thought they were overreacting. Others had called it a dog. Just a dog. A dog with hellish blue eyes.

She looked behind her again. It growled as something began to unfurl along its spine. Wings. She watched open-mouthed as blue-veined bony wings spread over the beast's back. The beast flew to the farmhouse and circled around it before it flew back to her and perched on her shoulder. Its snout rested on Grete's head as her hair grew wet with drool. The beast gripped her neck in its front claws and sank its hind claws into her arms. She cried out in pain. I must go on, she whispered to herself, but if giving up had been a respectable choice, she would have died there and then. The beast grew in size, becoming heavier and heavier the closer she got to the farmhouse.

Her family watched Greta's plight through the window. One of her sisters held a candle, and Grete looked at their faces, praying that they would give her strength. Her father's face was pale with horror, her mother's with disbelief, while her younger sisters looked as if they wished they could run outside and help her carry the weight of the beast. Grete averted her gaze from the front door when she saw that her family's eyes all had one thing in common. Disappointment.

They continued to watch. Grete thought that if the beast grew any bigger, it would break her neck. The dark sky gradually started to become lighter. She was almost at the door when the winged dog sniffed her hair and dug its claws deeper into her skin. The beast flapped its wings, creating a small whirlwind until Grete finally collapsed. She looked up. The dog flew high into the air, howling and barking as it quickly shapeshifted into a hawk. The bird was a giant at first but grew smaller in size until it perched on the windowsill of her bedroom.

"Are you okay, my darling?" Grete's father carried her inside. They brought her tea, and her father promised that a slice of ham would give her back her strength. It didn't. Her sisters tried

to cheer her up by putting their hands into their socks and pretending that they were princesses traveling to a castle that floated in a sea of shimmering diamonds. When her sisters started to ask who the beast outside was, Grete's mother told them to be quiet. Her father carried Grete upstairs after her sisters had been tucked in.

"The beast," she said, "it's on the windowsill. Get it away from me, get it away, please."

"There's nothing here," her mother opened the curtain and pointed to the empty windowsill before she closed it again, "go to sleep. No harm will come to you here," she gave Grete a kiss on the forehead and left the room. Grete didn't dare to close her eyes. She thought she would never sleep again. She heard her mother opening the oven door in the kitchen, and when the smell of yeasty bread entered her room, she fell asleep. The aroma meant home. It meant she was safe.

***

When she eventually woke up, it was late in the afternoon. Her father was repairing an old clock at the kitchen table.

"Ah, my sleeping rose has awoken," he said cheerfully.

"That beast…" Grete said, "is it still out there?"

"It's too early for talk of beasts," he said, pouring some tea and pushing a plate with a slice of bread and butter towards her. "Eat."

"Why aren't you furious with me?"

"You're here and unharmed," he said, "what's there to be furious about?"

"Something must be done. That beast. We can't be prisoners in our own home as soon as night falls."

"The horses need to be fed. That's the only thing that needs to be done."

Grete would have preferred to stay inside. Though her back still ached from carrying the beast across the field, she went to the stables. They had five Brabant horses. Alfie was first. She stroked his forehead and filled its bucket with hay. In the next stall, she admired the long black hair on the lower legs of a gray horse. Something wasn't right. She felt as if she had known this horse for longer than she had been alive, but yet, it was the first time she had ever seen the animal. She looked into its eyes. They weren't brown as they should have been but bright blue with dazzling irises that enchanted Grete. She felt as if those eyes had been born in the veil of white mist where spells are born. She opened the stall and led the horse out of the stables.

170

Its rose gray coat sparkled under the fading late afternoon sunshine. She touched the animal's neck. She had never known a horse to feel so soft, so velvety and warm.

The horse remained silent, but as soon as Grete mounted, the stallion suddenly started to gallop. She clung to its mane, terrified that she would fall off. Her legs gripped the sides of the horse as she had been taught to do, but it still didn't slow down. She cursed herself for not slipping a bridle on the horse before riding it. She watched in dread as they rode away from the farm and entered the forest.

"Stop!" she shouted, but the horse refused. The tree trunks that blocked parts of the path in the forest failed to slow the horse down. Grete started to calculate what her chances of survival would be if she jumped off the horse's back. Suddenly, the stallion reared up, sending her sprawling into a moss-covered pond, where she soon found herself swarmed by thousands of buzzing mosquitoes. A water vole sitting on a stone goggled at her. Grete stood up and climbed out. The horse was a horse no longer. It was now a black bird once again. The bird laughed in the same manner a human would. A guffaw that reveled in the horror she had been through. It was the beast.

***

Twenty years later, Grete had still not told her family what had happened when she rode the horse that wasn't supposed to be in the stables, but from that day forward, she refused to go anywhere near the horses. Any mention of the beast was strictly forbidden in the house, but it was still all Grete could think of.

She asked travelers about the beast and eventually learned that his name was Kludde. After her father passed away, she visited many farms in remote villages and inns in dense cities across Flanders. Her small notebook didn't suffice, and she soon had written hundreds of pages with tales of people who had had the misfortune of meeting Kludde.

The shapeshifter didn't just appear in the guise of dogs, birds, and horses but also bats, toads, and even trees and plants. Many reported having seen him in the shape of a dog, and some said they heard him before they saw him. Kludde was known to carry a chain with him that made a horrendous rattling sound and was attached to his paws. When he appeared as a horse, he enticed people to ride on his back, only to then throw them into rivers and ponds. Yes, he loved to force people to carry him, but he was also responsible for a couple of deaths. Kludde sometimes crawled close to people who were sleeping. He would then grow in size and suffocate them. He not only lurked in woods, cities, and fields, when Grete visited people who lived near rivers and creeks, many said they avoided the water, for that's where Kludde was known to be a waterdevil.

Not many could tell her what Kludde actually was, but they did know where his name came from—Kludde screams Kludde when he finds himself in an unpleasant situation. It was only after Grete met an old shepherd that she learned more about Kludde's origins. He had once been a farmer who had made a deal with the devil in exchange for wealth. He lived a life many could only dream of for twenty-five years, and after that, his time was up. His soul now belonged to the devil, and the farmer was doomed to walk this earth for all eternity without ever being allowed to form any friendships or find any peace. Did the shepherd know where this farm was? No. But he had heard it was called *Hellehoeve*. Grete's eyes widened. Her family's farm was called *Hellehoeve*. Kludde was her ancestor.

ALVERMANNEKES

Blaas dat licht daar eens uit! Blaas het uit!
Wij willen geen kijkende gezichten, wij
Willen dat hun ogen dicht zijn! Donker,
donker, donker! Zij die ons bekijken
krijgen een eeuwigdurende
*duistere nacht!**

Werkertje dragged the woman over the hill. He was glad they had stuffed an old rag that reeked of rotten fish entrails and dill in her mouth. He didn't want to hear her screams or, worse, her sobs while she begged him not to do what he was about to do. Werkertje tightened the rope around her wrists and feet and spat in her thick brown hair.

Three days ago, they had knocked on her door. They had told her they were alvermannekes. They had said they were happy to do her laundry in exchange for porridge and they had been very clear that there was one thing she must never do: watch them as they work. And what did the human giant do? She snuck out of bed in the middle of the night and watched them as they slapped her clothes clean against the rocks in the river. Yes, she was a spy, and every alvermanneke knew that spies must be punished.

Werkertje pushed his shovel into the ground and began to dig a hole. He wondered if one foot into the ground would be deep enough. Or two? He paused. *Filthy little gnome.* That's what she had called him when he caught her spying. She hadn't apologized. Oh no, she was too good to say sorry. She had mocked the red hat he wore, of which he was so proud, and then she had started to run. She had said that he would never catch her with his stumpy legs. He didn't have to. She tripped over a broom and knocked herself unconscious. Yes, one foot would be enough. Werkertje loved to work, but this woman didn't deserve more of his sweat than was absolutely necessary. These hills were far removed from human society, and he doubted anyone would hear her screams even without that old rag in her mouth.

He shoved the woman into the hole and smiled when he saw the fear in her eyes. He hoped that the sun would burn her skin and that the crows would start eating her flesh before she was well and truly dead.

Werkertje walked back to the woman's cottage. Lopertje was waiting for him.

"Is it done?" he asked.

"Let's leave this place," Werkertje said, "and hope we can find an honest human to work for."

The two alvermannekes said farewell to the wooden cottage and the tulips and pansies in the garden. They had been in this world for much longer than humans, and Werkertje still remembered the days when people were only preoccupied with hunting and gathering. Oh, how blissful that time was! He had never thought humans would learn how to grow crops and eventually build castles and cities. There wasn't anything special about humans, but these giants had won this earth just by the sheer number of them walking on the surface.

The alvermannekes had been content living in their underground holes for centuries, but then the day came that humans ruined everything for them—as they had done with so many other species. They had built a church next to their hole, and the constant ringing of the bells had made their home uninhabitable. Now, they had no other choice but to enter this dishonest world and work for despicable giants who called themselves humans.

Werkertje and Lopertje walked for quite a while until they stumbled upon a farm that looked as if it could do with some extra help. The alvermannekes offered to harvest the wheat at night in exchange for meat. The farmer readily agreed and promised not to spy on them. Though there were only two of them, they got more work done in one night than the many other farmhands in seven days. The first night, there was a very tasty steak with pepper sauce waiting for them. The second night there was another delicious steak but without any sauce. The third night they had finished harvesting all of the crops and ate dinner while they sat on the haystacks.

"I'm so old that I have seen an oak grow from an acorn," Werkertje said, "but I have never tasted such inedible flesh."

Lopertje looked around him. The cows were quietly staring into the night in the far distance, and a lone hare leapt in the bare fields. The alvermannekes' eyes widened when they heard a strange sound. Werkertje replayed the sound in his mind. Yes, it was the sound of boots walking in the mud.

"It's not meat," Lopertje said, "we're eating an old shoe sole."

"I see," Werkertje threw what the farmer had tried to pass off as meat on the ground, "blow out that light over there."

Lopertje blew into the air, and a cloud of mist left his mouth. The farmer fell into the bushes and crawled toward the two alvermannekes on his hands and knees as he cried out.

"How does it feel, farmer?" Werkertje asked, "with no light in your eyes?"

"Give me back my sight, and I'll reward you. This farm and everything I own will be yours. I promise. Just give me back my sight."

"Murderers are locked up, so they can't murder anymore. Spies lose their sight, so they can't spy anymore," Werkertje said, "that's how it works, farmer, you'll get used to it."

"You know what I'm sick of?" Lopertje's face had turned red, "these cursed giants. Humans are pests. Have you ever known even one of them who keeps their promises? I think not. And then there are those damned churches everywhere. How they don't get headaches from that horrendous ringing and clanging is beyond me."

"I quite agree," Werkertje said, "we'll be better off leaving this world."

The sun had already gone up, and the two alvermannekes enjoyed watching the farmer screaming as he struggled to find his own front door in a darkness only visible to him. Once they got tired of that, they said farewell to the cows. They bowed to the bluebells, the beeches, and to the ladybird that crawled on the leaves as they walked through the forest and to the sea. It was said there was an entrance there that would take them to a place without giants. Werkertje wondered if there would be woods and mountains in this other world. He wondered if once all of his kind had found their way to this giantless world, gates could be built to close the opening and prevent humans from following them. For if they found out…oh, if they found out… they would build more of those damned churches again!

*Blow that light out over there! Blow it out!
We don't want faces that watch, we
want their eyes to be closed! Dark,
dark, dark! Those who watch us
suffer an everlasting
dark night!

FLABBAERT

Forgive me, Father, for I have sinned. It's been eleven months since my last confession. Before I confess my sins, you must know who I am, for only then will you understand the gravity of my offenses against God.

I'm an ordained priest and have been working in the same parish for fifteen years. As you doubtless know, the church is discouraging superstitious beliefs amongst our worshippers, and as a priest, it is my duty to reprimand those who toss salt over their shoulders. In this village, this has proved to be an impossible task. Superstitions are ingrained not only in the souls of the parishioners but in the very landscape itself. Water from a nearby spring that is believed to be holy is often used by villagers to sprinkle on their windows when there is a heavy thunderstorm. They say this simple act will stop any damage from occurring. Children are only allowed to look into a mirror with an adult present, for they believe that if the child grimaces, the devil will appear and slap the child in the face. One time, the parents of a child I was about to baptize even asked me if I could make the baby cry loudly, for they wanted their son to be a good singer when he had grown up. Needless to say, I preached against these superstitions, but the parishioners paid me no heed.

As the years went by, I eventually found myself nailing a horseshoe over the door. I accepted a pouch containing the bones of a hanged thief to bring me good luck that was gifted by a lady who was worried that something awful might befall me. I even bought potions and concoctions to ward off evil spirits from those who were too proud to accept charity but had no bread to eat. But that isn't my greatest sin. Oh no, I committed my greatest sin when the bully of the town was murdered. He excelled in putting people around him down and instigated more than one fight in the inn simply because he was bored. There was nothing he found more entertaining than watching two people punch each other in the stomach and break each other's noses. He was a despicable cockroach. A stain that needed to be eradicated…oh God, forgive me. I must not be wrathful or speak ill of the dead, but he made my blood boil, and I would have committed the murder myself if someone else hadn't beaten all of the life out of him before I had the opportunity.

Flabbaert murdered him. He's a ghost who has haunted the parish for over one hundred years. Yes, a ghost. I hear you sigh at the other side of the confessional, but I will not discuss the existence of ghosts with you, for I have seen more than one with my own eyes, and my eyes don't lie. Flabbaert was a red, fiery ghost who was said to have died when his house burned to the ground. He often flew around the town at night, scorching his handprints on wooden doors. You would think the villagers despised him for ruining their doors, but they didn't. They viewed it as a work of art, something unique that no other village had. There was only one man who didn't agree. That bullying cockroach. He mocked Flabbaert whenever he saw the ghost. He threw rocks at him and hit him with iron poles. One night, Flabbaert had had enough. He dragged the man to the river and started to drown him. While the man's arms flailed in the water, Flabbaert dragged him onto the riverbank. There, he repeatedly hit him until every bone in the man's body was broken.

I was happy to hear he had died. I was happy to know that the children could walk to school without having insults hurled at them and that the villagers could hang their laundry outside without fearing it would be smeared with pig excrement. I admired Flabbaert. He had rid us of the pest that turned our

town into a place of torture, and therein lies my greatest sin. I celebrated the death of a man and took the side of an unnatural being who should have no place in this world. The family of the man demanded that Flabbaert be punished. I wanted the ghost placed under my protection. I wanted him to have a home in the church. There wasn't much Flabbaert could do as he consisted of flames and would have to be careful not to touch anything, but I wanted him to be my friend. Unfortunately, I had no other option but to punish him for murder. I banished Flabbaert to the sea, where he must remain for one hundred years. I think of him every day and the terrible fate I have bestowed on him while I could not stop smiling as the bully was lowered into his grave. And I'm so angry, oh, I'm so, so angry. How many Hail Marys will you have me say?

FLERIS

Vincent walked through the fields. Only two years ago, ten people had been harvesting cabbages and onions. It was September, and this year, carrots and radishes should have been growing on the farm, but aside from a lone magpie perched on a barren tree in the far distance, there wasn't a soul around. His land, the land he had inherited from his father and that had been in his family for centuries, had become a wasteland. Not even chickwood or crabgrass would grow here.

Vincent was unsure who was to blame, but he still remembered the day a young lad knocked on the door of the farmstead like it was yesterday. It was the day everything changed.

"I'm looking for work," the muscled lad said.

"Quite a lot would be required from you," Vincent said, "spraying and harvesting crops, maintaining the fences, and milking the cows. There's also work that needs to be done at the mill, but I must admit you look like you can handle it."

The lad introduced himself as Fleris and said, "you won't be disappointed."

Vincent thought there was something not quite right with Fleris. Though he kept himself to himself, there was a mean streak in his eyes. He also refused to sleep in the bunkhouse and slept on a haystack in the cowshed instead. Fleris claimed he felt more at home with the animals. Since he soon proved to be the best farmhand Vincent had ever had, he let the lad do whatever he wished.

Fleris did not bring harmony to the farm. One of the other farmhands claimed that he had seen Fleris sucking the blood out

of a cow. Vincent had dismissed it as evil gossip, but he began
to have doubts when he witnessed Fleris strangling a chicken
with one hand and eating its raw organs, heart, and liver —all
while baling hay with the other hand. Yet, the farm prospered
while Fleris was in his employment, and Vicent was willing to
close an eye to Fleris' weird habits as long as the farm
continued to flourish.

But the priest had a different opinion. How the old man in the
village found out was a mystery, but when the priest heard that
Fleris had discouraged people from attending mass and invited
them to gambling parties where much beer was poured, he
demanded that Fleris be fired. Vincent said no. He wasn't going
to let his best farmhand go. The priest informed him that Fleris
transformed himself into a black horse to get so much work
done. Vincent laughed. He didn't believe it and even if it was
true, he didn't care as long as the work was done in time.

That was before the catastrophe at the mill. One day, as the
mill was grinding grain into flour, all of a sudden, the flour
turned red. It was no longer flour. It was human flesh and blood.
Vincent was suspected of murder. The authorities ransacked his
farm as they searched for corpses or bits of fingers in the sheds,
cellars, and even his bedroom. There was nothing to be found,
but that didn't prevent them from accusing Vincent of being a
deranged murderer who wanted to make some extra money by
selling human flesh to the butcheries. And what did Fleris do?
He nearly choked on his own laughter.

Vincent had had enough. He reluctantly went to the priest and
asked him for advice. The priest said Fleris wasn't a farmhand.
He wasn't even human. He was a devil. And if Vincent didn't
banish this devil his farm would fall to ruin. The priest gave him
instructions and Vincent did what he knew he must the
following morning.

"Here's your breakfast," he said to Fleris.

"Porridge with garlic?" Fleris grabbed a chair and slammed it against the wall until it broke in two. He clenched his fists and stared into the farmer's eyes. Vincent thought that he was about to die. If anyone's eyes had the power to strike someone else down in a rageful fit, it was the eyes of his devilish farmhand.

"Porridge with garlic?" Fleris repeated, "Porridge with garlic? Fine, I'm leaving, but the good luck will leave too."

To Vincent's surprise, Fleris left without wrecking anything else. He had lost his best farmhand, but he was relieved that Fleris was no longer there. Besides, thanks to the hard work of this devil the farm was doing so well that he could afford to pay the wages of five extra farmhands. Yes, he believed that his farm would continue to thrive.

Then, the crops failed. The cows stopped giving milk. The chickens stopped laying eggs. Slowly, it started to dawn upon Vincent exactly what Fleris had meant when he had said that the good luck would leave, too. He returned to the priest and asked him for an explanation. He had, after all, claimed that his farm would fall to ruin if Fleris stayed. The priest told him his farm was doomed the day he hired Fleris. It didn't matter if Fleris stayed or left, but it was good that that devil no longer lived in their midst, for he would have brought so much more misery, sinfulness, and pain. Vincent wasn't so sure. He blamed the priest for the wasteland his farm had become. He would never have given Fleris that damned bowl of porridge with garlic if he had known that the priest was spouting harmful schemes that only benefited The Church and now all Joost could do was cry, cry, cry in the fields that used to be his livelihood until he slowly but surely went mad.

Lange Wapper

I'm the Lange Wapper, giant,
shapeshifter, and the drunkard's nightmare.
Whoopee! And tonight, tonight I will
be dancing around the tombs with glee!

Do you see what I see? Oh! It's a horrendous sight! There are no drunkards about. There's nobody to follow and nobody to torment. There's nobody whose head I can smack with a mallet

or push down into the overflowing sewers. Booooooooooooring!!
Oh, take pity on your poor giant, all alone in the darkness.
There's so little light. The other creatures who lure the people of
Antwerp to their deaths at night are creeping through the streets
with little luck, and I want more light. More deadly light, I say!
Oh, no, no, no, no, it can't be quiet, I can't be sullen and
miserable. I want glee! I want to laugh and sing! Gleeeeeeee!

*The daughter of a shoemaker lives
in Vlaeykensgang, beautiful is she and four
suiters has she, and tonight I felt
ladylike and became she for her suitors
will prove their love to me.*

Yes, that's what I did! I want to be loved. They say love is so
beautiful, oh so very beautiful, and those who are in love walk
on clouds and have butterflies fluttering in their bellies. It's an
experience that surely nobody wants to deny me? I want
butterflies! Many, many butterflies! We'll see, yes, we'll see
how much they love me. And soon, yes, soon, for I'm walking
now past the cathedral that is smaller than me to the graveyard.
My suitors will come. I've never been frightened of graves; it's
a very silly thing to be afraid of, but I've heard humans are, and
oh, how I love their fear! But will they love me? Will they
follow my instructions? We'll see!

*The first bell tolls, and my first suitor
sits on the largest cross in the graveyard. The second
bell tolls, and my second lover lies in the
coffin underneath. The third bell tolls, and my
third suitor knocks on the coffin. The fourth
bell tolls, and my fourth lover walks around the
cross with a heavy chain. I have a daisy. Do they
love me? Do they love me not? Do*

they love me?
Love me truly?
Forever and ever?
Till death do us part?

Knock! Knock! Knock! Oh, do you
hear? Whoopee!! Knock! Knock! And
I cackle and cackle and dance with glee!
Gleeeeeee! Do you hear the chain? It rattles and
clatters! But the best sounds are yet to come!
Hear! Oh, hear! The screams! Their lovely,
lovely screams!

My first suitor falls from the cross and
dies when my second lover crawls in the
coffin. My second love dies from
fear when the third one knocks on the coffin. And
then my third suitor scares himself to death when the
rattling chains announce doom! Dooooooooom!
Oh, dear, whatever shall I do? Dance with
glee! With glee! With glee! Gleeeeee! But
what of my fourth suitor? Hihihihi. He
goes to the river and drowns himself. For
how can he live? Being guilty of
muuuuuuuuuuurder!! Yes, yes, unwittingly and
without intent, but muuuuuuuuuuurder!!
Tralalalala! And I dance once more with
glee! Wheeeeeeeeeeeeeeee!

Oh, what a night! What a perfect night! Death and darkness are
light to me, and there was so much light I almost became blind!
They all loved me! And they didn't just love me a little —they
died out of love for me! How deeply they cared! How
considerate and thoughtful of them to turn this dull night into

one I will treasure forever, and think back on with unrivaled happiness and gleeeeeeee! Whoopee!

***

But not long after, the wrong kind of light entered my life. The people of Antwerp discovered my biggest fear. Sculptures of the Virgin Mary. Bah!! They're a ghastly sight! She's evil! Innocence and purity! It's evil! Evil, I say! Effigies of that sickening lady were soon placed everywhere in the city, and I was driven out of Antwerp. There was no more glee. Only sadness and despair and wretchedness. A trait I loved seeing in humans but not in me. Oh, no! Not in me. My home was no longer my home. I fell into a river and drowned. But I was one of the lucky creatures, for at least I knew what it felt like to be loved! Oh, those lovely, lovely butterflies!

LODDER

You want to know of strange things that have happened around here? *Ben je zeker?* Alright then, I've got a story for you. Thirty years ago, I was at a wedding, or it might have been a wake, a christening even. I don't exactly remember, but that's not important, what is important is that it was late when I returned home. Now, you might expect me to tell you what the house looked like. Well, it was a squalid building, and I won't go on and on about it *of we zitten hier volgend jaar nog.*

I'm not going to tell you how visible the stars were, what phase the moon was in, or if it was raining or not—it doesn't matter. Anyway, it always rains in these parts. What does matter is the sound I heard when I put my key in the keyhole. It was an odd noise, as if someone was raking cobblestones out of the ground. So I looked behind me, and there was nothing. A deserted street. That was all there was to it—but then I saw it. A silver pocket watch lying in the middle of the road. *Dat is geluk hebben!* Some doctor or lawyer or *één van die opgeblazen kevers in een das die niet weten hoe te zwijgen* must have lost it. The watch would pay my rent for the next six months, so I did what anyone would have done and put it in my pocket.

I went to my room. Nothing out of the ordinary. *Één groot rommelboeltje zoals gewoonlijk.* It had become a habit of mine to sigh at the filthy clothes piled in the corner. So, I sighed. Then I closed the curtains, and as usual, they were so dusty they made me cough. Normally, I would crawl underneath the blankets, but I had something to admire that evening. The watch. I wanted to study its engravings underneath the oil lamp before I took it to the pawnbrokers in the morning. So, I put my

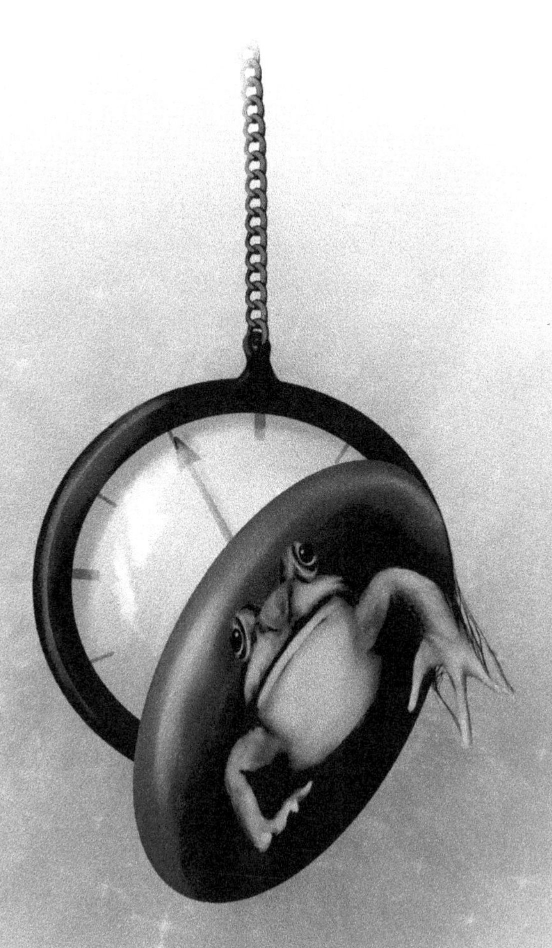

hand in my pocket, and you know what it felt like? A clump of ice! I took it out of my pocket, and guess what I was holding? Not a watch, oh no, no, no, no, not a watch, a toad! It was bigger and had more bumps on its repulsive green skin than toads usually have. Bah! A girl I grew up with had once kissed a toad, and her face was covered in warts the next day. I was afraid that touching it would condemn me to the same fate, and so I did what anyone would do—I threw that little troll against the wall. A dead toad. That's what I wanted to see. But *nee godverdomme*, that's not what happened. That's not what was there. It was a dog! A black dog! The toad had shapeshifted into a mongrel with red eyes that glowed like lanterns. It stared at me, and it wouldn't look away. Not even for a second. And if I have to be an honest man, I admit that I was hoping it would look away so that I could run off like the coward I was in those days. *Schrik! Schrik! Schrik*! But instead, I stared right into its eyeballs for I don't know how long, hoping that it would understand that I wouldn't go down without a fight. My legs trembled violently, and I thought that day was to be my last, the day I would bid the earth *vaarwel*. Oh, farewell trees, and the raggedy inn where I spent most of my waking hours. Just when I thought I was going to faint and be ripped into shreds, my curtains moved aside without anyone's help, the window opened itself, and the dog jumped out. I thought that the mongrel must be dead or, at the very least, injured. But no, I ran to the window, and there it stood in the middle of the road, laughing himself half silly. *Nondedju.* That's when I knew who it was. Lodder. A loathsome little thing he is. Can shapeshift into anything he likes, and he loves to paralyze with fear all those who have the misfortune of meeting him. There's no length he won't go to to give someone the shivers, but the one thing he'll never do is kill. *Gene moordenaar maar een verdomde kwelduivel.* I've tried to find out where he comes from and how to banish him to the sea or a rock or tree where he can do no

more harm, but nobody knows how. One thing's for sure: if I
ever meet him again, it will be the other way around. He'll be
the one who's trembling. *Dat kan ik u verzekeren.*

ENDNOTES

In this chapter, we visit the unique beings who dwell in
Flanders's folklore realm and begin our journey with the story
of a creature shrouded in mystery, Kludde. He's known far and
wide for his uncanny ability to shapeshift into dogs, horses, cats,
birds, bats, toads, and even plants and trees, though he prefers to
take the shape of dogs and horses. In most tales, he's a
mischievous being who forces people to carry him and does
little harm, but according to other stories, he has been
responsible for suffocating people. The reimagined tale has
attempted to include everything we know about this delightfully
evil being, including his origins while showing the fear that was
associated with Kludde through the character of Grete.
Alvermannekes are gnome-like figures who are known to do the
laundry and other household work in exchange for food. In
many tales, they are regarded as kind and helpful beings, and
nothing goes wrong, but because conflict is necessary in any
story and they hate being spied upon, this reimagining is
inspired by two folktales in which things do go wrong. In the

first, a woman is dragged to a hole and left there, and in the second, they punish the onlooker by blowing out the light in his eyes. These were the two ways in which Alvermannekes took revenge on those who spied upon them, with the latter appearing in the majority of folktales. Many stories say that Alvermannekes eventually left Flanders because they were heathens and couldn't stand the sound of church bells. Flabbaert is a fiery ghost who was said to dwell here and murdered his bully. According to the original folktale, a priest reluctantly banished him to the sea, reluctantly because he seemed to have had more sympathy for the ghost than for the bully. The superstitions mentioned in this story are also real superstitions that were once believed in Ostend. Fleris is the diabolical farmhand who loved mischief and discouraged people from going to church. When he was served porridge with garlic, he left the farm and took good luck with him. In the next tale, we meet a giant called Lange Wapper, who is a folkloric figure who is still very well-known in Antwerp. As with so many other Flemish beings, he's an excellent shapeshifter, and in the tale that was chosen, we see him at his most evil and quite mad. Eventually, the people discovered his greatest fear, and in Catholic Flanders, this, of course, had to be effigies of the Virgin Mary. It's often said he's the reason why there are so many effigies of her in Antwerp. We end this book with the tale of Lodder in which a couple of Dutch sentences are included. Lodder is, again, a highly skilled shapeshifter and trickster, but he is basically harmless. While he loved to prank and terrify people, he never did any actual harm.

Acknowledgments

Axel Kallesøe

Angelika Pia Schmid-Riley

James M.

Jessica Retherford

Rachel D.

Alex

Felisluna

Damien Fialkowski

Sophia A.

Kerry Stubbs

Majda G.

Nico C.

Keir F.

Aline Lonneville

Jenna

Wren Collier

Jo Price-Murray

Aleksandra Brokman

Erin Louttit

Colleen Feeney

Matt H.

Ricky

Mark R. West

Laura S.

Solomon Stone Romney

Lisa Fryer

Anton D.

Michael DeCuypere

Johannes Rehborn

C.R. Shelidon

Valerie Linzner

Stefan A.

Neil Byrne

Muriel G.

Lea Mara

Seamus Sands

Zack Fissel

Sara Kaufman

Oskari S.

Nick Moore

Natasha Rueschhoff

Catelynn W.

Jo Westman

Charlotte E. English

Kaas

Christopher P.

Paul Herkes

Nancy B. Kleinert

Kameron Claire

Rossano De Santis

Christopher Brooks

Chee L. W.

Elizabeth Kiefer

Jolie M.

Mary-Ann Thorson

Holly Herda

Betsy J

Jay Kiser

Alexis Hope

Ihor Markevych

Kipstje

Douglas Wisteria Wren

Ollie Oxxenfree

Charlotte B.

Mr H00t

We are indebted to the folklorists who collected these folktales and preserved them for future generations.

Alfons de Cock (1850-1921)
K. C. Peeters (1903-1975)
J.R.W. Sinninghe (1904-1988)
Hervé Stalpaert (1914-1981)
William Henderson (1813-1891)

And Vlaamse Volksverhalenbank
(https://www.volksverhalenbank.be/)

www.ingramcontent.com/pod-product-compliance
Lightning Source LLC
Chambersburg PA
CBHW040139160726
48006CB00014B/1545